# CHRISTINA'S
## TRIBULATION
BY – RAYDON COOLEY

# CHAPTERS

1------NO LOOKING BACK
2------MY GRANDBABIES
3------THE AWAKENING
4------A HOME FOR THE HOLIDAYS
5------WASHINGTON
6------NEW COMPANION
7------LESSONS TO LEARN
8------CABIN IN THE MOUNTAINS
9------BIG RED DOG
10----FARM HOUSE
11----RENO NEVADA
12----CHRISTINA'S DAUGHTER
13----BONDING TIME
14----MY NEW DAD
15--THE BIG PLAN

# CHRISTINA'S TRIBULATION

## PROLOGUE

Christina lived an average childhood. Born and raised in Erie Pennsylvania. Her father was the preacher, and a horse breeder. Her family has a beautiful beach house down in Texas, where Christina spent her summer vacations with her older sister, Sera. At the age of twelve, the world starts to unraveled. Civil Society has begun to be converted into radicals. The United Nation was deployed worldwide.

At the age of fourteen, Christina's older sister Sera was eighteen. Sera was drafted by the New U. S. Police and sent to Seattle Washington to help with the unrest. One year later is when the electromagnetic pulse attacks happened, and it destroyed electricity worldwide.

**THE U. N. OUTLAWED ALL RELIGIONS.**

Christina and her parents were forced to flee their home. Christina was sixteen at the time her parents were killed by the rogue "U.N. DEMON'S." That is what her father had called them. Her parents had decided that they had to sacrifice themselves in order to save Christina. Then she was left all alone, except for her horse.

## "BLACKWALL."

The last words her dad said to her were "GO AND FIND YOUR SISTER" This begins Christina's quest to track down her older sister Sera. "NEVER FORGET WHO YOU ARE" was what Christina's mother's final words were to her, and Christina took her mom and dad's very last words to heart. With her horse BLACKWALL Christina's long journey begins.

She heads down toward Texas to their beach house, trying to stay out ahead of the rogue U. N. DEMON'S, and crazy renegades. Most of the people have killed each-another, and civilized people were few, and far between.

## WHISPER YOUR NAME
### By – RAYDON COOLEY

ONCE AGAIN YOU'RE SWEET VOICE IT WOKE ME.
AS I REACHED TO HOLD YOU ONCE AGAIN.
THEN I REALIZE I WAS ONLY DREAMING.
LYING HERE ALONG IN MY BED.
THEIR WILL COME A TIME.
WHEN WE'LL BE BACK TOGETHER.
UNTIL THEN.
I WILL TRY TO KEEP SANE.
WHEN I FIND.
THAT MY MIND BEGINS TO WONDER.
I'LL JUST STOP.
**AND WHISPER YOU'RE NAME.**
THERE ARE TIMES I FEEL I'M GOING CRAZY.
I HAVE DREAMS OF YOU TIME FROM TIME
I MISS YOU SO MUCH THAT IT PAINS ME.
YOUR DEAR LOVE IS ALWAYS ON MY MIND.
THERE WILL COME A TIME.
WHEN WE'LL BE BACK TOGETHER.
UNTIL THEN.
I WILL TRY TO KEEP SANE.
WHEN I FIND.
THAT MY MIND BEGINS TO WONDER.
I'LL JUST STOP.
**AND WHISPER YOUR NAME.**

# CHAPTER ONE
## NO LOOKING BACK

Christina is sixteen years old; five feet seven in. tall, one hundred ten lb. and still growing. She has long full wavy blond hair and sky blue eyes.

Her and her parents have been on the run for the last two years. After fleeing their home up in Erie Pennsylvania, they are now hiding out in a small group of warehouses just fifteen miles south of Oklahoma City, Oklahoma. The U. N. DEMON'S begin to move in on the building where they were hiding. Christina's father and mother knew that there was no escaping. They decided to make the ultimate sacrifice, in order to try and save their youngest daughter. Her dad turns toward Christina and tenderly takes her face between his shaking hands. With tears streaming down both of their faces, her dad begins to speak.

*"Sweetheart you must listen to me, O.K.; you take the thoroughbred and you go south as fast as you can; go to the beach house and wait for a short while. If your mother and I do not show up in a week or two, I want you to go north-west, toward Seattle Washington.*

*That is where they took Sera; you take off and find Sera. Now pay attention to me Christina; do not look back; you hear me. DO – NOT – LOOK – BACK!!"*

Christina's dad told her, as she buried her face into his wide chest and wrapped her skinny small arms around his large body and held on tight.

Christina's mom pulled Christina away from her dad's firm grip and squeezed her little girl tight into her bosom. Then she gave a nod to dad so to let him know the U.N. DEMON'S are out front. Mom lifted Christina's face and held it between her two hands and gave Christina a loving kiss on her lips.

*"Never forget who you are."*

Christina's mom whispered through her tears, as they stared into each-other's eyes.

Christina's mom pushed Christina up onto the back of the black thoroughbred, BLACKWALL.

Mom slowly pulled the sliding door on the back of the warehouse open and took a peek outside, and then turned to look at dad. When dad opened the front door and then turned, giving mom a quick nod; she slapped BLACKWALL on the butt as hard as she could. Unsuspecting the sudden sting, he leaped into a fast run out through the back door and headed south. He reached out with his front legs as far as they would go, and pulled large chunks of real-estate up under himself and pushed it out behind with his large powerful hind legs. Being only a little bit over two years of age and still a bit wild, all Christina could do was hold on as tight as she possibly could, and do her very best to keep from falling off, until BLACKWALL ran out of breath.

    Christina could hear the gun fire behind her. She wanted to stop and turn around and go protect her parents, but there was no controlling this young solid black horse, as he quickly ate up the landscape at a hard run.

    Later that evening as the sun was sinking in the west, Christina guided BLACKWALL toward a small trailer house that was slightly hidden in a group of trees. They both were exhausted from the days ride, and from all of Christina's constant trembling and crying all throughout the day. BLACKWALL could since the sorrow and the fear resonating from Christina's body, and he realized that he was left with the responsibility of keeping her safe.

*"Who the hell are you?"*

A female voice asked loudly, as BLACKWALL came to a stop.

The teenager jerked on the rein trying her best to make her horse turn and flee, but BLACKWALL stood still, refusing to move. Christina rocked hard back and forth in the saddle and kicked the horse, in the attempt to force BLACKWALL to run, but he refused to budge.

*"I asked, who the hell are you?"*

The female voice asked loudly; standing with her bow-and-arrow pointing at Christina.

Christina was staring at the tip of the arrow with large eyes, her ears began to ring loudly as the world began to spin all around her; everything suddenly went completely black as Christina fell, hitting the ground with a hard thud. BLACKWALL lowered his head and gently gave Christina a nudge with his nose, and then looked up toward the woman.

*"Well shit!"*

Debby exclaimed, setting her bow down on the deck that was attached to the front of the trailer.

Debby is a widow woman in her early sixties. Six ft. tall with long black hair; and well built. Her husband had passed away a few years earlier, and with no children, she now lived alone.

Debby carefully picked up the dirty, skinny teenager and carried her up the steps and into the trailer; laying the young girl onto the couch she covered her with a light blanket.

Christina was completely exhausted from the tremendous tensions of the day's events, and she slept sound throughout the night.

Christina was woken by the morning sun as it seeped in through the small living-room window. She rose up onto one arm and looked all around the well kept room. Christina notices a large glass of clean water sitting on the coffee table. She quickly sat up and grabbed the glass and downed the cool water, and with trembling hands she slowly sat the glass back onto the table.

*"Good-morning young lady."*

Debby softly said, from the other side of the breakfast bar that divided the kitchen from the living-room.

Christina quickly turned her head to see who was speaking. She saw this pretty older woman standing in the kitchen, over a hot stove, flipping pancakes. She realized that the air was filled with the delicious aroma of frying bacon. Christina set frozen with big eyes, watching Debby slowly walk around the breakfast bar toward her with outreached hands.

"*Come on sweetheart, you need to eat.*"

Debby explained to Christina, reaching and pulling the skinny teenager to her feet and in the direction of the kitchen table. Christina quietly followed, still in a daze from yesterday's event.

"*I'm not really hungry.*"

Christina softly whispered, watching as Debby sit the plate full of hot pancakes and crispy bacon down on the table in front of her.

"*No ma'am, you are going to eat.*"

Debby demanded, taking a small jar of fresh honey from the cupboard.

Debby took pride in her honey; honey that she gathered herself from her bee-hives. She set the jar down on the table in front of the tall skinny teenager.

"*BLACKWALL! Where is BLACKWALL?*"

Christina loudly asked, quickly looking up toward Debby with a concern look on her face.

*"Your horse is fine; he is tied up out behind the house."*

Debby explained, sitting a cup of hot coffee in front of Christina.

Debby pointed at the plate full of pancakes with a gesture that said eat, and then took a seat across from Christina. As Christina began to slowly eat, her body's need for nutrition took over and she started to eat the pancakes faster and faster, until the bottom of the plate was completely visible. Debby and Christina set quietly for about five minutes, than Christina began to speak.

*"Mom and dad died yesterday, saving me; I don't know what to do."*

Christina said with a shaky voice, with tears streaming down her cheeks.

*"I am very sorry for your loss; this world has gone to hell; many, many people are going to die. You have no choice sweetheart, you must grow up quickly; and by quickly I mean now."*

Debby explained; standing and moving over beside Christina and gently wiping the tears from her cheeks with her rugged farm hands.

*"Daddy told me to go and find my sister Sera; so I have to go find Sera."*

Christina said in a daze, leaning into Debby and completely going limp from the confusion of the situation that life had put her in.

*"O.K. babe, you come with me, I'm going to put you in the extra bed-room and you can rest until tomorrow; I will gather up the things that you will need to survive."*

Debby said, helping Christina to her feet and keeping her balanced.

Christina wrapped her arms tight around Debby as if her life was depending on it. They slowly walked down the hall and into the extra bedroom. Debby lovingly removed Christina's shoes and socks and put her under the covers, gently kissing her on top of the forehead as she caringly pushed Christina's dirty hair from her face.

*"Thank you."*

Christina whispered, as if it took all of her energy just to speak.

*"You're welcome sweetheart, now you get some rest."*

Debby said with a smile, softly closing the door behind her.

The rest of the day and through-out the night, Christina would dose off to sleep; then suddenly wakeup from the nightmares of U.N. DEMON'S terrorizing the world. When she was lying awake between sleeping, she would consider what Debby had said to her about the growing up now thing; and she knew that it was true.

Christina lay in the bed watching the daylight seep in through the window from the morning sun. She became frightened at the prospect of leaving and trying to survive all on her own. She slowly put on her socks and shoes and started down the hall toward the kitchen.

*"How are we feeling this morning?"*

Debby asked, pouring Christina a cup of coffee as she took a seat at the table.

*"O.K. I guess, my name is Christina, and I don't know how to hunt; what I mean is; I don't know how to survive."*

Christina whispered, staring down into her cup of coffee.

*"Well shit! I guess you will be staying for a while; I will teach you a few tricks on how to survive; my name is Debby."*

Debby agitatedly said, putting breakfast onto a plate, and then sat it down in front of the fragile teenager.

"You said that I have to grow up now, but I miss mom and dad so much; so I need you to teach me how to grow up."

Christina said, with tears running down her cheeks, as she began cutting into her pancakes.

"I do believe that you are going to be just fine sweetheart, just fine."

Debby said, looking across the kitchen table as Christina began to eat her pancakes and sip on her coffee.

For the next four weeks Christina paid close attention as Debby taught her survival skills. She practiced endlessly on the art of the bow-and-arrow. Debby taught Christina the best way to climb up a tree and scout for danger and how to build a fire pit, and which wood to use; keeping it small so not to attract attention. Debby made sure to showed Christina her wind-mill.

"You keep your eyes out for these things, every-body are now building these for water."

Debby told Christina, as she showed her how to work the wind-mill.

Christina spent every evening brushing and talking to BLACKWALL; *"It will bound the two of you together"*; Debby told her.

Christina woke-up this morning as the bright light from the sun shown in through the bedroom window, proud that she now has the skills and ability to survive on her own. Christina slowly got dressed and then walked down the hall toward the kitchen with sadness, as the aroma of frying bacon filled the air, she knew it was time for her to leave.

*"Good morning pretty lady, how are we feeling this morning?"*

Debby asked with a loving smile, as Christina poured herself a cup of coffee.

*"O.K. I guess; Debby, it's time for me to go and find my sister."*

Christina said quietly, taking her seat at the kitchen table.

*"Yes ~ yes I know."*

Debby sadly whispered, turning and looking at Christina with water filled eyes.

Christina quickly jumped to her feet and ran to take Debby into a tight hug as tears streamed down their faces; they had become very fond of each-other over the last few weeks.

*"I will never forget you, and it might be a few years, but I promise you, I will come back and visit you."*

Christina promised, through her crying breaths accompanied with tears, with her skinny teenage arms wrapped tightly around Debby.

*"I will always be here, now sit and eat."*

Debby said, releasing Christina from her grip and turning to stare out the kitchen window with tears running down her face.

After breakfast Debby helped Christina saddle and pack the supplies that she had gathered, upon the back of BLACKWALL. Debby stood out on her deck with tears drifting down her face, watching Christina ride away on the back of BLACKWALL with every-thing that she would need to survive. Christina's tears streamed down her face as she rode south toward her family's beach house, and began her quest to find her sister Sera.

# CHAPTER TWO
## MY GRANDBABIES

Christina kept BLACKWALL at a fast pace for the next week. Not only because she wanted to get to the family beach house as soon as possible, but it also kept her mind from missing her mom, dad and Debby. She was becoming very accurate with her bow-and-arrow that Debby had given her, and the art of the hunt. Mid-day Christina decided it was time to take a short break; she climbed a tall tree to scout the aria. As she was sitting up in the top of the tall tree looking all around through her binoculars, a chill ran down her spine.

*"What the hell is this?"*

Christina asked herself, copying a phrase she had heard Debby say many times.

Christina could see smoke rising up from a small fire. She focused her binoculars and slowly looked around the camp. She spied two small children sitting next to a small tent. She could make out that the smaller one was a long haired girl that looked to be around ten years of age, leaning up against the larger boy who looked to be around thirteen years of age. He was gently rocking her side to side as if he was trying to give her comfort as she held onto him tight.

"*Well shit.*"

Christina proclaims, slowly shimmying down the tall tree; again copying Debby's language.

"*BLACKWALL, we have to go and see if those two children need our help.*"

Christina explained, sticking her foot in the stirrup and mounting BLACKWALL, then heading in the direction of the children.

Christina cautiously rode into their camp looking all around. Both of the children were nowhere to be seen. She set for a moment and then dismounted. Suddenly the sound of a babies crying caught her ears; she concentrates on where the sound is coming from. Christina turns her attention toward the small tent. Her eyes became as big as silver dollars when she looked into the tent to see a small baby that looked to be about five months old.

"*Get away from her; get away from her!*"

A tiny weak voice attempted to scream.

Christina turned to see a tiny three foot tall skinny little girl swinging a small stick around in the air, running fast to protect her baby sister. Christina reached and easily took the stick away from the small girl and pulled her into a tight embrace.

"*I'm not going to hurt you; I want to help.*"

Christina said, holding a firm grip on the small girl as she wiggled, trying to get away.

'*Please don't hurt my friend.*"

A voice said, as a young boy stepped out from behind a large tree.

"*Damn-it all to hell; I'm not going to hurt you, I want to help. My name is Christina, now come and talk to me.*"

Christina explains, with a few new words that she had recently learned mixed in.

She gently picked the tiny girl up in her arms and stared at the small boy. The small boy stood and stared back at Christina as the tiny girl kept one arm around Christina's neck and turned to stare at the boy with Christina.

"*O.K. I'm going to believe you; my name is Wesley and you are holding Sharon, and Lisa is her baby sister.*"

Wesley conceited, gradually walking toward Christina.

Sharon squeezed her arms as tightly as she could around Christina's neck and began to weep. Christina began to carefully walk around swaying back and forth and hummed a soothing tune trying to comfort the tiny girl.

"O.K Wesley, where are your parent's?"

Christina asked softly, continuing to rock Sharon back and forth in her arms.

"DEAD!!"

Sharon said loudly, into Christina's ear.

"Shit, shit, shit."

Christina whispered, with another one of her recently learned phrases.

Christina watched Wesley slowly walk past her and Sharon and enters into the tent, returning with Lisa wrapped in his arms and attempting to quiet her crying, copying Christina's motions.

"Let's make her some honey-water."

Christina suggested, carrying Sharon over toward BLACKWALL to retrieve the jar of honey.

"You have honey; can I have some honey-water to?"

Sharon asked with excitement, keeping one arm wrapped around Christina's neck, looking toward BLACKWALL.

*"Yes you can sweetheart, we will all have some honey-water."*

Christina giggled, taking a jar of honey from the saddle-bag and giving it to Sharon as she set her down.

*"Look Wesley, look, we have honey."*

Sharon informed her older friend.

Sharon held the jar tightly against her body so not to drop her precious cargo, as she carefully walked toward Wesley.

Wesley reluctantly handed Lisa over to Christina, and then he took the jar of honey from Sharon. Christina could not help but smile, watching Sharon bouncing up and down, watching her young friend mixing the honey into a small canteen of water. Wesley filled a tin cup up with the sweet water and handed it to Sharon first, and then he filled a baby bottle. Wesley carefully retrieved Lisa back from Christina and gave the baby her bottle. Lisa's eyes became big with pleasure as she began sucking down the sweet treat, as Wesley gently rocked her. As Christina looked around the camp she noticed the small deep pan sitting beside the fire pit with brown water in it, and a few bugs floating on the top.

"O.K. kid's, I'm going to go get something for dinner; can I trust you to leave my things alone?"

Christina asked, taking her bow-and-arrows and hunting knife from the saddle.

"YES! We were taught not to touch other people's things."

Wesley exclaimed, as if Christina had just insulted him.

"O.K. it's my turn to trust you."

Christina said, turning and heading off into the woods.

"So we don't have to eat bug soup tonight?"

Sharon asked, looking up at Wesley as she sipped on her container of sweet water.

"No Sharon, I do believe that we will be eating real food tonight."

Wesley said, taking Sharon's hand as he watched Christina disappear into the forest with her bow-and-arrow.

"I like Christina, she seems nice."

Sharon said, leaning up against Wesley and gently rubbing Lisa's short blond hair.

"Yea, I like her too."

Wesley said, watching as Lisa faded into a peaceful sleep as she finished her bottle.

Sharon went into the tent and brought out a blanket and laid it in the shade. Wesley laid Lisa down and then turned to Sharon.

*"I'm going to go and get some firewood; I need you to watch Lisa."*

Wesley told Sharon, as he turned and started toward the woods.

*"Wesley, you don't need to tell me that; I know it's left up to you and me to raise her."*

Sharon told Wesley, taking a seat down on the blanket beside Lisa.

*"Yea; I guess we have to grow up fast, HU."*

Wesley said, turning back for a moment and giving Sharon a smile.

*"YEAP."*

Sharon said point-blank, as she lay down beside Lisa.

An hour later when Christina returned with three rabbits and three squirrels, some wild onions and potatoes she had found growing; she found Wesley, Sharon, and Lisa, sleeping on a blanket beside the small pile of wood that Wesley had gathered in anticipation of a good meal. Christina would occasionally glance over at the trio that were sleeping as she prepared dinner.

*"Something smells great."*

Sharon said, rising up and looking over at Christina cooking dinner.

"You can wake up your brother, dinner is ready."

Christina told Sharon, removing the food from the fire pit.

"He is not my brother, he is my boyfriend; Wesley wake up, we don't have to eat bug soup tonight."

Sharon exclaimed, shaking Wesley hard; as hard as she could.

"Wait; you have been eating bugs?"

Christina asked, with a bit of surprise in her voice, tilting her head and giving Sharon a look of disbelief.

"Yea, like forever."

Sharon answered, sitting beside Wesley and staring at Christina with anticipation of the real food.

"Well let's eat and then I will explain what I have come up with for you three."

Christina said, and then handed Sharon and Wesley their plates.

After the tasty meal vanished, Wesley and Sharon began the cleaning of the dishes. Christina began to give BLACKWALL his gentle brushing. Sharon left Wesley to finish the dishes and stood quietly by and observed every tiny move that Christina made. Sharon followed behind Christina and watched as Christina set up her screen tent that Debby had given her.

*"Wow, your tent is so cool; can I sleep with you tonight?"*

Sharon asked, trying her very best to help Christina set the tent.

*"Yes sweetheart, you may."*

Christina answered, with a slight giggle.

*"O.K. Christina, what do you have planned for us?"*

Wesley asked, holding Lisa in his arms.

Wesley rocked Lisa back and forth; giving her another bottle of the sweet-water with a bit of mashed potato mixed in. Lisa stared up at Wesley as she sucked down her sweet fulfilling treat. Wesley lovingly returned her stare as he waited for Christina's answer.

*"Well Wesley, it's getting close to dark and the mosquitoes are starting to coming out, so we will talk tomorrow."*

Christina suggested, as she and Sharon were finishing sitting up the screen tent.

*"O.K, I will see you in the morning."*

Wesley said, standing and taking Lisa into their tent for the night.

Sharon had an uncontrollable giggle as she and Christina climbed into the tent and lay down. Sharon cuddled up close against Christina and wrapped her arms around her as she listened to the soothing sound of Christina's humming.

After a sound night's sleep with their full bellies, the sun began to peak up-above the horizon. Christina was awakened by the crying of a baby. Christina lay still staring up at the blue sky with Sharon's arm across her belly, as Sharon snuggled up-under her arm. Christina got a big smile on her face as she heard Wesley making a bottle of sweet water for Lisa. Christina began to fantasize about being all grown-up and having her own daughter. But being only sixteen, she knew that was far into the future.

*"Momma! Momma! Momma! Where are you Momma?"*

Sharon screamed through her tears, as her body began to tremble.

*"Hay, hay babe; everything O.K."*

Christina quickly whispered, wrapping her arms around Sharon to give her comfort.

*"Christina, please don't leave us alone, please."*

Sharon shouts, climbing onto Christina with tears flowing from her eyes and with her body still trembling.

*"I will never leave you alone, I promise."*

Christina assured Sharon, rocking her side to side; wondering if she was doing it right.

Christina quietly began to sing a lullaby, as Sharon settled and drifted back off into a sound sleep. Christina carefully covered-up Sharon and then quietly slipped out of the tent. She retrieved all the items that Debby had given to her for making pancakes, even a big bag of home-made powdered mix. She put some small sticks into the fire-pit and then began mixing-up some of the mix. Christina had a few pancakes cooked and sitting to the side when Sharon stepped out from the tent. Sharon froze into place for a moment, looking at Christina in amassment.

*"WESLEY!! WESLEY!! Wake up! Wake up! We have pancakes! We have pancakes!"*

Sharon shouted, running as fast as she could toward the tent that Wesley and Lisa were in.

*"Yes Sharon I know, I have been watching."*

Wesley said with his chuckle, stepping from the tent with Lisa in his arms.

"O.K. come and eat."

Christina said, finishing the pancakes and setting the hot pan to the side, and then she reached and took Lisa from Wesley.

Christina felt a little bit grown-up, sitting with Lisa in her arms and watching Sharon and Wesley gobbling up their hot pancakes with honey poured all across the top. After breakfast and after the dishes were put back into their rightful places, Christina set between Sharon and Wesley.

*"Listen kid's, here is my plan; about a week's ride north, there is this lady named Debby, she is like a Grandma~."*

Christina was explaining, when Sharon quickly interrupted.

*"I love Grandma's; Grandma's are always cooking."*

Sharon said with excitement, wrapping her arms around one of Wesley's arms.

*"Yes sweetheart, she cooks all the time; now she lives alone and I'm sure she would love for you three to live with her. So I'm taking you to her house."*

Christina finished saying.

*"Can we leave today?"*

Wesley asks, putting one of his arms around Sharon and holding Lisa with the other.

*"Yes sweetheart we can, but your horse is small and you will need to down-size quite a bit; so let's get started."*

Christina said, than she stood and started over to their tent.

Wesley gently handed Lisa to Sharon and followed Christina. They began their work as they listened to Sharon's tiny sweet voice singing soft lullabies to Lisa. When everything was sorted and packed up onto the back of the horses, they mounted up and headed north toward Debby's little obscured trailer house that's nicely tucked away in the tree-line. Sharon could not stop smiling as she settled into Christina's lap way up high on the back of BLACKWALL. Lisa babbled with content in her small homemade baby carriage that was securely fastened onto the back of Wesley's small colt. On the second day into their long journey north, Christina realized that with two small children and a baby, it was going to take her much, much longer to return to Debby's house.

Christina began to teach Wesley how to sit very quiet and very still for long periods of time; the most important part of the hunt, and wait for the animals to come out of hiding, then dinner was in the bag.

Sharon demanded on sleeping inside the screen tent with Christina almost every night; she would snuggle up against Christina's side and fade off to sleep. On the seventh day into the trip, they came across a few head of goats playing in a big field. Christina spotted a mother goat with two small kids. Christina eased Sharon down beside Wesley, and then she and BLACKWALL began slowly circling the momma goat, when the goat charged Christina roped her hind legs, and then she quickly jumped down and looped her small rope around the goat's neck, and her front feet. Being raised on a horse ranch was now coming in handy. The mother goat gave in and stood still. Wesley and Sharon stood far off and watched in amazement.

*"Bring me your deep pan."*

Christina ordered, as she retrieved her deep pan from the back of BLACKWALL.

Wesley and Sharon slowly and cautiously crept up alongside Christina and the subdued goat. Wesley set the pan down beside Christina. He and Sharon watch Christina as she began milking the momma goat. Sharon giggled as she watched the pan being filled one squirt at a time.

*"Take this and fill Lisa's bottle, and pour the rest into your canteen."*

Christina told Wesley, quickly switching out the full pan for the empty one.

With both pans and a canteen filled with milk, Christina slowly untied the goat and they watched as she ran to her two kids waiting in the distance and disappeared into the forest.

*"We will set camp early so that we can enjoy our prize; over there in those trees."*

Christina said, pointing toward a thick part of the trees, along the tree-line.

After they had the horses unpacked and camp was set, Sharon set with a big smile on her face as she held Lisa's full bottle of goat's milk, watching Lisa gobbling it down.

*"O.K. kid's, I'm going to go get dinner."*

Christina said, retrieving her bow-and-arrow and hunting knife.

*"Can I come with?"*

Wesley asked, quickly standing up and staring at Christina.

*"Yes. Yes you may."*

Christina said with a smile, impressed with Wesley's willingness to learn.

Christina was taking Wesley out for his first real hunt. After walking a short while, they settled down inside a thick bunch of bushes next to a small stream of running water that was about four feet across and only six inches deep. Wesley had learned to breathe in and out slowly and not to move a muscle. Wesley had the bow up and ready when they saw a young buck strolling up to the stream. Christina took a deep breath, praying that Wesley didn't miss. Wesley let loose of the arrow. The two pointer never seen the arrow flying at him through the air; the arrow hit just behind the right front leg, plunging through the skin and into the heart, causing the deer to drop instantly.

*"Steak tonight."*

Christina said with a smile, as she stood and started toward the deer with her hunting knife in hand and with Wesley close behind.

*"That's gross."*

Wesley exclaimed, watching as Christina cut strips of meat from the hind quarter of the deer.

*"No. No Wesley, its survival."*

Christina corrected Wesley, and then she stood and handed him her hunting knife.

*"WHAT! You want me to do that."*

Wesley asked, with a raised voice and big eyes, as he reluctantly took the knife.

*"Yes Wesley, you are the one that shot him; and I will not always be here for you, so you need to learn how to survive; I mean, you don't want Sharon and Lisa to be eating bugs, right."*

Christina explained, taking a step back and pointing to the deer.

*"O.K. ~ O.K."*

Wesley whispered, slowly stepping up, and began to carve strips of meat from the deer.

Wesley and Christina returned to camp with a pack full of deer meat, Wesley quickly began to build a small fire in the fire pit and then he helped Christina prepare the meat; proud that he had played a major part in the supplying of dinner for his younger girlfriend. Every once in a while Sharon and Wesley would glance at each-other and give a wink and a smile. Christina could not help but giggle to herself at the sight of the two. After dinner they all sat around the fire-pit and Christina sang a few familiar songs that she could remembered listening to before all of the earth's electricity was eliminated. Wesley and Sharon enjoyed the entertaining evening that Christina was providing them. When the mosquitoes began to attack, Sharon climbed into the screen tent with Christina. Wesley took Lisa into his tent. They all slept sound through-out the night, with full bellies. Even Lisa had her fill of goat's milk.

A few days of riding had past when they came upon a slow flowing river that was about one hundred feet across and five feet deep in the center.

*"How about fish for dinner tonight?"*

Christina asked, looking down at Sharon, as Sharon looked up with a smile.

*"Are you going to go fishing?"*

Sharon giggled, with excitement in her voice.

*"No. You are going to fish."*

Christina answered, and then lowered Sharon down to the ground.

*"WESLEY!! WESLEY!! I'm going fishing."*

Sharon exclaimed, skipping over toward Wesley with a happy bounce in her step.

Christina dismounts from BLACKWALL, and then she and Wesley started to unpack the horses and set camp as Sharon set with Lisa in her arms watching. After camp was all setup, Christina retrieved the fishing hooks from her saddle bag with the spool of fishing string. She cuts two small limbs from a tree, and made Sharon and Wesley their own fishing-poles. Then she moved a dead tree trunk that was lying on the ground as Sharon and Wesley watched close to every move that Christina would make.

*"O.K. kids, both of you catch one of the worms."*

Christina said, and then she watched the two quickly pick up the worms.

*"This is how we make bug soup."*

Sharon explained to Christina, holding the worm up.

*"Well fish love to eat worms, now let me show you how it goes on the hook."*

Christina said, trying her best not to let the picture of eating bugs enter into her mind.

Christina took Sharon's worm between her thumb and her fingers and threaded the hook through the center of the worm, as Wesley and Sharon was watching closely.

After Christina was finished, Sharon quickly took her fishing-pole to the edge of the river and tossed the hook into the water. Wesley carefully put his worm onto his hook and followed suit. Christina set between the two holding Lisa with a smile of content on her face; letting her mind play the game of being a grown-up, and a mom, as the teenager held the bottle of honey water with Lisa snuggled in her arms. Lisa sucked down the sweet water, as they stared into each other's eyes.

*"I got one! I got one!"*

Sharon excitingly screamed, quickly standing and walking backward.

Sharon had to use all of her strength to hold the pole up into the air; dragging the flopping fish out of the water and onto dry land. The fish seemed to be very hungry today, as Wesley and Sharon pulled in one after another, making their very first fishing experience almost magical. Christina took Lisa and laid her into the small crib, and then took some string from a small spool and made a stringer and showed them how to fasten the fish onto the stringer, and then Christina began to gather-up fire wood while the two caught their fish. Lisa was sleeping sound inside her small crib as Christina built the fire pit and started the fire. Wesley and

Sharon were laughing as they constantly ran back and forth to the rotten log for more worms. Christina kept a watch on the two as she gathered up the utensils that they would need for cleaning and cooking the fish.

*"We can't find any more worms."*

Wesley explained, with disappointment in his voice, as he and Sharon came into the camp.

*"O.K. how many fish do you have?"*

Christina asked with a smile, watching Wesley carrying the two poles and Sharon dragging a string of fish.

*"We have twelve!"*

Sharon quickly answers, before Wesley had the chance.

*"Wow, you can count."*

Christina said, taking the string of fish from Sharon.

*"No, Wesley told me."*

Sharon shyly said, turning her eyes down at the ground.

*"Well I bet if you asked Wesley, he will teach you how to count."*

Christina said, giving Wesley a sweet smile with raised eyebrows.

*"Will you Wesley? Will you please teach me how to count?"*

Sharon begged, grabbing onto Wesley's arm and looking up into his baby blue eyes with her bright brown eyes.

*"Yea, I can do that; just because we are going to be together like forever."*

Wesley said, giving Sharon a tight hug, as he smiled up at Christina.

*"O.K. you two, come with me and I will teach you how to clean and cook the fish."*

Christina said, turning and heading back toward the river with Sharon and Wesley close behind.

Every chance that Wesley had he would practice with the bow-and arrow, and he has begun to get really good with the art. Christina had taught Sharon how to bathe Lisa and make her bottles. Christina was very satisfied with herself as being grown-up and caring for others. It has been three weeks since Christina had found the two children and before the end of this day, Wesley, Sharon, and Lisa would be meeting their new Grandma Debby.

Christina began to lean forward in the saddle causing BLACKWALL to pick up the pace; Wesley ordered his pony to keep up.

Sharon became very excited as Debby's little trailer came into view.

"*Grandma's house! Grandma's house!*"

Sharon enthusiastically shouted, while wiggling around on Christina's lap.

Debby stood out on the deck in front of her house looking through her binoculars, impatiently watching as Christina and the small children were slowly approaching. She put down her binoculars, and quickly went down the steps to meet Christina and the children in the front yard.

"*What the hell is this?*"

Debby asked, reaching up and carefully taking Sharon as Christina carefully handed her down into Debby's waiting arms.

"*I found these kid's about three weeks ago; their parents are dead, and bringing them to you was the only thing I could think of.*"

Christina explained, as she dismounted and then gave Debby a big hug.

Sharon wrapped her arms around both of their necks and squeezed with her loud giggle, with butterflies dancing around in her belly.

Debby quickly set Sharon down; staring in disbelief as Wesley walked up with Lisa wrapped in his arms. Debby gently took Lisa from Wesley's arms, and then turned and carefully started up the steps and into the front door with tears slowly drifting down her face as she kept her eyes locked onto the small baby.

"*I think Grandma is in shock.*"

Christina said, taking Wesley and Sharon by the hand and starting up the steps.

Debby was sitting in her rocking chair softly humming a tune, still entranced with the presence of the small baby when they entered through the door. Debby looked up for just a second.

"*Christina; go out to the barn and milk the cow, this baby needs milk.*"

Debby told Christina, and then looked back at Lisa and resumed with her humming tune.

"*I'm going to help.*"

Wesley demanded, following Christina out the door.

Sharon stood and stared at Debby, taking in every one of her features. Debby looked up and gave Sharon a warm smile.

"*Are you going to be our Grandma?*"

Sharon cautiously asked, gazing up into Debby's eyes as she rubbed her sister's hair.

"Yes, I can be your Grandma, now what do I call you?"

Debby asked, stopping her rocker and reaching up, gently putting her hand against Sharon's tiny cheek.

"My name is Sharon and my baby sister's name is Lisa."

Sharon answered excitingly, reaching up and taking Debby's hand into hers with a big smile on her face.

"And what is your brother's name?"

Debby asked, moving Lisa over to one side and pulling Sharon into her lap, than continued her rocking.

"He is not my brother, he is my boyfriend, and we are going to get married some day, he promised me so; his name is Wesley."

Sharon explained, with her eyes beginning to get heavy from the constant rocking.

"O, I see."

Debby said with a smile, continuing with her gentle rocking.

Debby began humming a soothing tune as the two girls faded off into a peaceful sleep in her arms.

Christina and Wesley entered the small barn that was completely covered-up with vines and bushes, almost unnoticeable from a distance.

*"Let me, I need to learn how to do this."*

Wesley said, taking the milk bucket from Christina.

Wesley slowly walked over to where the cow was waiting and squatted down, placing the milk bucket under the cows utters.

*"Just like you seen me milk that goat."*

Christina said, watching as Wesley set down and nervously began to fill the bucket one squirt at a time.

*"Christina; I realize that you will not be staying, so I want to say, thanks for saving Sharon and Lisa."*

Wesley softly said, staring at his hands as he milked the cow.

*"You are welcome Wesley, but I don't think I did all that."*

Christina said with her shaky teenage voice, knowing Wesley was sincere with his words.

*"Yes! Yes you did Christina; we were really starving. We were raised in the city, all I knew was playing video games, and then the electricity went out. My dad explained to me about all the crazy things that are going on in the world, then one day about two months ago he and Sharon's dad put us in the secret underground room behind the house and told us to stay in the room for at least three days before we came out. We were so scared Christina. When we came out, both of our parents were laying in the back yard dead. Everything had been taken; I mean like all the food. So we started walking through the wood, trying to keep hidden and find thing to eat. The camp we were in when you came, we had just found a few days before you found us. The man at the camp was dead so I used his horse to move the body away. I promise you, I will learn to survive. I love Sharon, and I plan to marry her some day. So thank you."*

Wesley said, standing up with his half a bucket of milk in his hand.

*"My parents died saving me to Wesley, and I believe you are going to do great."*

Christina said, taking the bucket of milk from Wesley and sitting it down onto the ground, and then she embraced Wesley as tears seeped from her eyes.

Debby was still sitting in her rocking chair softly humming a tune when Wesley and Christina came through the door.

*"Christina, take Sharon and put her in the extra bedroom."*

Debby whispered, as she leaned forward so Christina could take Sharon from her lap.

*"I will go bring Lisa's crib in."*

Wesley said, putting the bucket of milk on the kitchen table and heading out the door.

Christina quietly put the tiny girl into the bed in the extra bedroom and set down beside her, than hummed a soothing tune until she faded back off into a deep sleep. Christina returned to the kitchen and smiled at Debby, setting with Lisa and humming a soothing tune.

*"I will make Lisa a bottle of milk,"*

Christina said; reaching into her small pack and retrieving a clean bottle.

*"Christina; I never had children, and when Steve passed away a few years back I was left alone. I was so glad when you showed up last time, and so sad to see you leave; I am*

*so proud of you for caring for others, and now I have Grandbabies. Thank you."*

Debby said, setting and watching as Christina make Lisa a bottle.

*"You don't need to thank me Debby; the last thing mom said to me was;* **never forget who you are;** *and helping others is what my family was all about. I was just doing what I was raised to do. Now you know that I will be leaving tomorrow, right?"*

Christina explained, walking into the living-room and handing Debby the bottle.

Wesley came through the door with Lisa's small crib and placed it next to the small wood heater.

*"Yes sweetheart, you may go and find your sister; I will take good care of the children."*

Debby said; standing and placing Lisa in her crib with a warm bottle of fresh milk.

*"O.K. Wesley, You and me need to go and unpack the horses."*

Christina told Wesley, and then started out the door with Wesley right behind.

When Christina and Wesley had both of the horses safely tucked away into the barn and they returned to the house, Sharon had woke up and was now sitting at the kitchen table singing with her sweet sounding voice, entertaining Debby with her children songs as she watched her cooking dinner. Wesley quickly set down beside Sharon and joined in. Christina stood at the breakfast bar and smiled as she felt her mother's spirit fill the room. After dinner Debby sat in her rocker with Lisa, very impressed as Sharon and Wesley began cleaning up the kitchen.

## TIME FOR BED

Sharon and Wesley insisted on sharing the extra bed-room, and they demanded that Lisa's crib be put beside their bed.

*"I'm too excited to sleep; Wesley and me have a new Grandma."*

Sharon whispered, giving Christina a good-night kiss and tight hug around her neck.

*"Sweetheart I am so tired, I need to sleep."*

Christina explained to Sharon, as she tucked her in.

*"It's O.K. I'll read to her until she goes to sleep."*

Wesley said, picking up a small book from the dresser.

*"That will work."*

Christina said, than slowly closed the door and headed down the hall toward the soft couch that was calling her name from the living-room.

The next morning Christina was sitting at the kitchen table with Sharon sitting on her lap. Wesley sat with Lisa in his arms as she sucked down the fresh milk that Wesley had gotten from Miss Cow this morning; that's what he had named her; Debby was busy making breakfast.

*"Do you really have to go away?"*

Sharon asked disappointingly, staring into her glass of milk.

*"Yes dear, I have to go and find my sister, but I will come and visit, O.K."*

Christina explained, while giving Sharon a squeeze.

*"Yea; I understand, I love my sister to, just don't take too long."*

Sharon said, looking over at Wesley and Lisa, and then she continued to drink her milk.

After breakfast Wesley helped Christina pack up BLACKWALL, Debby gave her more supplies for her journey. Sharon set on the deck with Lisa in her arms and watched the ruckus.

Debby, Sharon, and Wesley with Lisa in his arms, stood out on the deck and sadly watched as Christina disappear into the distance.

# CHAPTER THREE
## THE AWAKENING

Christina has been riding south for three weeks, keeping BLACKWALL at his fast pace. Many times when she would come close to a small town, she would see the bodies of entire family's laying beside the road. The teenager tried her best to stay away from roads and towns as she made her way south toward her family's beach house. Which made the journey much longer than it should be. After a long hard day's ride, and a variety of new emotions, Christina decides that she will make camp early. She climbed a large tall tree with her binoculars so to scout the aria. Her tall slender teenage body begins to tremble at what she spies through her binoculars. On a back road off in the distance she saw two U.N vehicles and ten U.N. DEMON'S who have captured a family. Christina watches in horror as four of the DEMON'S dressed in U.N. uniforms tour the clothes off two teenage girls and begin raping them. When the father attempts to fight back, another DEMON shoots him in the back, and he dropped to the ground as his wife screams. Christina could not bear to watch this situation unfold any longer, knowing that she could not do anything to help the family. She quickly climbed down the tree.

*"We've got to go! We've got to go!"*

Christina kept repeating with a shaky voice, as she mounted BLACKWALL and started south.

With tears streaming down her face, and the images of what she witnessed playing over and over in her mind, she rode far into the night before stopping and setting up her screen tent. Christina left camp packed upon the back of BLACKWALL, concerned that the DEMON'S might come for her.

## ["DREAMS OF REALITY"]

Tonight Christina's dreams are so realistic she cries and screams out in her sleep. Her dream gives her short flashes of different images of towns and cities engulfed in fire.

Groups of people killing other groups, and then they would take the spoils. What few cars that were still able to run were out of gas; people with guns began to run out of bullets and abandon their guns.

Christina woke-up in a cold sweat and trembling breaths.

*"It was just a dream. ~ It was just a dream."*

Christina told herself, sitting with her head in her hands and taking in deep trembling breaths.

Christina sat in her screen tent until the sun had forced the mosquitoes back into the under- brush, than she carefully rolled up her tent and put it in its place. She climbed a tree and took a look around, and then she mounted BLACKWALL and headed south. Every couple of hours she would take a break and climb a tree to scout for danger. Christina realized that life on earth was no longer safe; {MANY, MANY PEOPLE ARE GOING TO DIE}; registered in her mind, as the image of Debby on that first morning replayed in her psyche.

After several more weeks of keen riding, and dodging many crazy gangs and U.N. DEMON'S, Christina was excited as she and BLACKWALL slowly crosses the deserted bridge that took them out to the beach of Surfside Texas.

*"We made it!"*

Christina exclaimed to BLACKWALL, with a bit of disbelief in her voice.

She put BLACKWALL into a gallop down the sandy beach toward her family beach house just a short ways down the beach, enjoying the gentle breeze that was coming off of the water. When she reached the house she quickly dismounts, and then tied BLACKWALL up-to the deck and flew into the house. The teen ran from room to room as if she truly expected to find mom and dad or even Sera waiting to greet her. After the second time of making the circle through the house, she slowly walked back out onto the deck.

*"Damn-it-all-to-hell."*

Christina softly whispered through her tears, as she set down on the steps and stared out across the bay.

Christina began to notice that there was no one around. She suspiciously looked all around and realized that many of the houses that had once lined the beach had been burned to the ground.

*"I have to grow-up now."*

Christina told herself, standing to go and begin the task of unloading BLACKWALL.

After everything was placed inside the house, Christina went into the kitchen and checked the five gallon propane tank and found it was still full. She quickly ran down to the storage room and found that dad's rod-and-reel was still where he had left it, along with the cast net; that was used for catching bait.

*"YES!! Fish for dinner."*

Christina shouted, heading toward the water with the fishing gear in hand.

Christina does her best to remember how her dad had taught her to throw the cast net, after many tries she begins to get the hang of it, and caught a few small croakers; small fish which are used for bait. She baits her hook and slowly wades out into the bay up-to her waist, and cast the rod-and-reel, and then she returned to the beach and settles down onto the dry sand and patiently waits to catch her dinner. She begins to build a sandcastle as she lets her mind drift back to when she and Sera would play out on the beach every summer when they came down on their vacations. Tears had begun to slide down her cheeks when she heard the tiny bell on the end of the rod-and-reel start to ring. Christina quickly jumps to her feet and begins the battle of reeling in the large fish.

After cleaning and preparing and eating dinner, Christina slowly drifts through the house looking at all the memorabilia that her mom had placed upon the whatnot shelves around the living-room, remembering when and where each piece had come from. She slips into her dads study as if she might get in trouble for entering into the room without permission. She began to rumble through her dad's office desk, **"YES"** she shouts as she pulls out a small laminated book that read [U.S. Atlas Map] from the bottom drawer. Lying under the map she finds his stash of new batteries in the bottom of the drawer. She quickly ran to her bedroom with the batteries in hand. Carelessly she began to pull things from her closet and toss them out onto the floor until she had found her small secret metal box. She quickly dug through her dresser drawer, tossing her clothes onto the floor until she found the key to the box.

Opening the box brought a big smile to her face as she pulls out her C.D. player and all of her C.D.'s. She quickly went down the hall and returned to the living-room. She put new batteries into the player, and then did a teenager flop down onto the soft couch, putting the ear-phones over her ears and listening to music until she faded off to sleep.

*"Christina. ~ Christina sweetheart,~ wake-up; Christina, wake-up sweetheart."*

A man's voice softly said, gently shaking her arm.

Christina woke-up with terror, causing her to rise up like a bullet and dash for the kitchen, dragging her C.D. player behind.

*"It's me Christina, It's me; Christina It's O.K., Christina it's me."*

The man said firmly, as he stood still and watched Christina come to a stop and turn to look at him.

Christina quickly turned when she recognized the man's voice. She stood for a moment and stared at a familiar looking older man in his late sixties, standing in the middle of the living-room, with a sidearm strapped to his hip.

*"Officer Jim! Officer Jim!"*

Christina shouted; running back across the room and into his arms, than she began to sob like the teenager she was.

"Where is your parent's sweetheart?"

Jim asked, holding the sobbing teen in his tight embrace.

Jim is a big man; six ft. five in tall; two hundred twenty lb.; he has now let his gray hair grow out, along with his beard.

"DEAD!"

Christina whispered, squeezing into his tight embrace, and burying her face into his massive chest.

"Sweet Jesus; I am so sorry sweetheart."

Jim said, softly stroking her hair, holding onto her with his other arm.

"Wait. Where is your wife Patty, and Jill; where is Jill?"

Christina demanded, looking up into his eyes with concern on her face.

"They are dead sweetheart, they are dead."

Jim softly whispered, as tears slid down his rugged cheeks.

"Many people are going to die."

Christina whispered with a sob, burying her face into Jim's massive chest.

Christina's mind began to reminisce about the summer days when she and Jill would play out on the beach with Sera.

Christina held onto her dad's best friend as he led her to the kitchen table. She has known Jim and his family her entire life. Christina set and watched as Jim put a pot of coffee onto the stove and then took a seat across the table from her.

"How did you know I was here?"

Christina asked with a calm voice, trying her best to be grown-up.

"I didn't Christina, I have been living here; my house was burnt down in the gang wars we had here last year."

Jim answered, taking in a deep breath so to calm himself.

"I am so sorry, how many people are left?"

Christina asked, as she began to notice how much Jim had let his appearance decline.

"It's just me sweetheart; I had to leave for a couple of months until all the fires burnt out, but it is just me."

Jim explained, standing and moving to the stove to pour them some coffee.

Christina and Jim sat and drank there first cup of hot coffee in silence. Christina's mind began to churn fast as she poured them their second cup of coffee.

"Jim, I have a good idea."

Christina said, setting Jim's coffee down in front of him and taking her seat.

"I'm listening."

Jim said, sipping his coffee as he noticed how grown-up that this sixteen year old girl had become.

Christina began to explain all about the situation of Debby and the children to Jim, and how they could really use his help.

"Why don't you want me to stay here with you?"

Jim asked, with a confused look on his face.

"I'm not staying here Jim, dad told me to go and find Sera; I'm going to be going up to Seattle Washington."

Christina said point-blank, with a look of determination.

"Christina, that is the stupidest thing that I have ever heard; not only is that dangerous, but it will take you around two years to get to Washington."

Jim said, giving a hard stare across the table at Christina.

*"It is dangerous everywhere, and I do not care if it takes me a hundred years Jim, I'm going to find Sera; now I need for you to go and take care of Debby and the children."*

Christina said with authority, as she stared across the table into Jim's eyes.

*"Let's set and visit for a few days, and we can discuss the situation."*

Jim said, standing and starting for the living room, when Christina grabbed onto his arm.

*"O.K. Jim, but do not even try to talk me out of going to find Sera; I'm going."*

Christina demanded, and then she stood and held tight onto his arm as they walked through the living room and out onto the deck.

Over the next few days Jim had began to realize just how lonely his life has been, living all by himself. After long discussions and deep consideration of his situation, Jim had decided to travel to Debby's.

*"O.K. Jim, here is my plan; we can travel together until we get to Summerville, so you can bypass Houston. You do not want to go

*through Houston, trust me. There is a lake in Summerville where we can take a break."*

Christina explained, as she and Jim studied the Atlas that she had found in her dads desk.

*"Sounds good to me."*

Jim said, as he and Christina copied out the directions that would take him the rest of the way to Debby's house.

Christina and Jim carefully pick out each item that they would be taking with them on their journey. Christina almost cried as she put her C.D player into the bottom drawer of her dad's desk; she knew the batteries would not last long enough to make taking it with her worthwhile, but truly hoped she would be back some day and listen to her music. With their horses all packed up Jim and Christina began their journey.

*"Horses love the soothing sound of singing and whistling."*

Jim explained to Christina, and he began to whistle a tune as they rode along.

*"I don't know how to whistle."*

Christina whispered, listening close to the tune that Jim was whistling.

*"Well then, I will teach you when we stop to camp, but for now we will sing a song that we both know. ~ Row – Row – Row your boat."*

Jim began to sing with a slight chuckle, as Christina joined in with a giggle of her own.

Christina and Jim sang happy children songs throughout the rest of day, which helped to pass the time. They were a little more than one-third of the way to Summerville when time came to camp for the night. After camp was set and dinner was finished, Jim and Christina sat by the small fire and laughed and giggled as Jim began to patiently teach Christina the art of the whistle. It did not take long before Christina was whistling along with Jim as she noticed the horses were paying close attention to their soothing tune. They sat until darkness had over-taken the light and the mosquitoes had begun to attack.

*"Screw this, I'm going to bed."*

Christina said, slapping herself in the face as she battled the mosquitoes.

*"O.K sweetheart, sweet dream."*

Jim said with a chuckle, climbing into the screen tent that he had brought for himself.

**[DREAMS OF HAPPINESS]**

Tonight Christina dreams about her sister Sera. Sera seems extremely happy and content, Sera hums a tune as she is preparing dinner for a man that Christina can't quite make out; but it is clear to see that Sera is very much in love with this man.

Christina was woken just at day-break. She set straight up with an intense scream as her ears began to ring from the loud gun shots that rang out.

*"JIM!! JIM!! Where are you Jim?"*

Christina shouts with a terrifying voice, than she sees Jim standing beside the horses with his long gun in his hand.

*"Pack up the horses Christina; quickly, pack up the horses."*

Jim demands, and then he fires off another shot.

Christina's adrenalin was flowing strong as she quickly packed both of the horses; occasionally glancing over at Jim as he scouted through the woods, looking through his scope that set upon top of his rifle.

*"O.K Jim, come on; come on Jim!"*

Christina yelled, sticking her foot into the stirrup and mounting BLACKWALL.

Jim quickly mounted his gray mar and they headed north at a fast run. Jim was constantly glancing back over his shoulder as they rode. As the horses slowed to a fast walk Christina began to speak.

*"What the hell was that?"*

Christina asked, between her long deep hard breaths.

*"There were three U.N. bastards."*

Jim whispered, keeping his eyes straight ahead.

*"U.N. DEMON'S; do you think they will follow us?"*

Christina asked nervously, looking back over her shoulder.

*"No Christina, those three bastards won't be following anyone again. As long as they didn't have any friend we are O.K."*

Jim answered quietly, still keeping his eyes looking forward.

*"Wait. ~ What are you saying; did you shoot them?"*

Christina asked with a squeaky voice.

*"I had no choice sweetheart."*

Jim answered, giving Christina an agonizing look.

After a long period of silence, Jim began to whistle a tune; Christina quickly joined in.{MANY PEOPLE ARE GOING TO DIE}, kept playing over and over in her mind as they rode along. Suddenly her mother's face streaming with tears flashed through her mind, {NEVER FORGET WHO YOU ARE}.

*"I love and miss you mom, I promise I will never forget."*

Christina softly whispers to herself, and then continued her whistling.

Every so often Christina and Jim would stop and climb a tree and scout for danger. Christina told Jim all about Debby, and how she had found Sharon, Wesley and Lisa as they rode along. Jim being a long time law officer and well trained in defense, would give Christina short lessens in defensive moves at each stop.

*"Remember this Christina, never trust anyone."*

Jim would say, after each lesson of self-defense he was teaching her.

Christina and Jim arrived at Summerville lake mid-day, as they rode through the small town they could see that most of the buildings and houses had been burnt down or rammed-sacked. As they rode toward the lake they saw just a few bodies lying here and there, but most people seemed to have fled.

*"Let's camp here for the night."*

Jim said, as they came up to the spillway in the center of the dam.

After staying at Summerville Lake for three days, two days longer than they had planned, it was time for them to go their separate ways.

*"Are you sure you don't want me to go with you?"*

Jim asked, after they had everything pack upon their horse.

*"No Jim, Debby and the children need you; I have a half a jar of honey, take the jar back to Debby; and I wrote this letter back at the beach house, please give it to Debby for me."*

Christina said, giving Jim the letter, and then quickly grabbing him and pulling him into a tight embrace.

*"I want you to take my hand gun; I have twenty bullets left."*

Jim whispered, holding Christina into a tight embrace.

*"NO!! I will never shoot anyone, that's not who I am Jim."*

Christina quickly said, pulling back and looking up into Jim's eyes.

*"You are a special woman, and all grown-up."*

Jim said with a smile, taking a step back and looking down at Christina, to take in a mental picture so to remember her.

*"Thank you Jim, I will see you in a few years; take care of my new family."*

Christina said, mounting BLACKWALL and starting back on her quest of finding Sera.

# CHAPTER FOUR
## A HOME FOR THE HOLIDAYS

It has been three months since Christina and her dads best friend Jim, have gone their separate ways back in Texas. Fall is now over and winter is setting in as BLACKWALL steps high, enjoying the cool breeze that is coming from the north. A few snowflakes begin to float through the air from the overcast sky.

*"You know what BLACKWALL? I do believe that it is our birthday."*

Christina told BLACKWALL, while she was pulling her sleeping-bag tighter around her body, trying her best to stop the cold air from seeping in.

Christina's mind began to drift back to her fourteenth birthday, when she and her dad help deliver her horse in the freezing snow up in Erie Pennsylvania, and how the small colt had slowed them down on their escape, her dad refused to leave him behind.

Christina begins to notice that all the high hill tops are now covered in snow. She knows that it will be prudent that she finds shelter for the winter, a place where she and BLACKWALL will be able to hibernate, and within the next few weeks.

*"I would like to make it into Oregon before we stop for the winter."*

Christina told BLACKWALL; she leans forward in the saddle, causing BLACKWALL to pick up the pace.

Christina pushed BLACKWALL hard the rest of the day, by late afternoon the wind had picked up and the snow had started to come down in large flakes. She came across a long high bridge that reached across a wide river. She led BLACKWALL up-under the edge of the bridge where the snow could not reach, and began to set up camp. She was now using her firm one-man tarp tent for the winter. After camp was set she retrieved her fish-hooks and fishing line from the saddle, than she pulled out the small package of spoiled squirrel meat that she kept next to BLACKWALL so it would not freeze. Christina found a small tree next to the river and tied the fishing line around the small tree, and put the rotten meat onto the hook and tossed it into the river. She began to pick up small twigs, smaller than her little finger. When she had an arm load of the small twigs, she returned them to the camp, now for the bit larger twigs. She kept this up until she had graduated to limbs the size of her arm and slightly bigger. She began with a small pile of tiny twigs as she started the fire. When the fire had reached a decent size and she had the larger limbs burning, she noticed the small tree that she had her fishing line tied to was wiggling.

"*YES! Fish for Dinner!*"

Christina said with excitement in her voice, as she headed toward the river.

After she had the three foot long cat-fish safely at camp, Christina headed for the woods to scrimp up some dried up grass for BLACKWALL'S dinner.

"*YES*"

Christina shouts out, when she finds a large patch of tall wheat-grass growing close to camp.

As BLACKWALL was munching out on his dry grass that Christina gathered for him, Christina cleaned her fish and sliced it into round pieces. As she cooked her catch of the day she whistled a soothing tune as BLACKWALL ate his treat with his ears perked up and enjoying the sound. After dinner Christina climbs into her sleeping-bag, still fully dressed and fade off into a deep sleep.

## [DREAMS OF MOM]

Christina is sitting by the fire when she sees her mother walking toward her from the edge of the woods.

*"Mom, your O.K."*

Christina shouts, as she stands and runs to takes her mom into a tight embrace.

*"Listen to me sweetheart, you must find shelter; and very soon."*

Mom says to Christina, holding her face between her hands.

*"Yes mom, I know it's getting cold; where is dad?"*

Christina asked, staring into her moms eyes with a big smile.

*"I have to go now, you find shelter soon."*

Mom said, as she turned and faded off into the forest.

*"No!! Come back; I don't want you to leave, please mom; come back!"*

Christina wakes up screaming for her mom to come back. She lay inside her tent with tears pouring from her eyes. Wishing she could hold her mom just one more time.

Christina slowly packed camp onto the back of BLACKWALL, watching the snow flurries drifting through the air.

*"We need to find real shelter my friend."*

Christina told BLACKWALL, sticking her foot into the stirrup and lifting herself into the saddle and starting through the snow.

Christina kept BLACKWALL at a steady fast pace. By mid-day the snow had stopped falling, but the breeze still had a negligible bite to it. BLACKWALL'S ears perked up as he moves his head in a slight up and down motion. Christina brings him to a stop so she can hear; the sound of turkeys gobbling filed the air. She instantly dismounts with her bow in hand. Christina moves behind some thick bushes and patiently waits for dinner to walk by. She has the bow up and ready when the turkeys come into view. Christina holds her breath as she releases the arrow and watches as it flies through the air.

*"What the hell is this."*

Christina shouts, before she thinks about the consequences that might be forth coming from her loud voice.

Christina set frozen in place feeling a warm sensation flow across her body as she stares at two turkeys with arrows sticking out of their sides lying in the snow.

*"Well I'll just be damned."*

A deep male voice softly said, coming from behind Christina.

Christina slowly turned to see an average size man standing several feet to the right and behind her next to a tree. She quickly stood and swung her bow in the direction of the man as she pulled back another arrow.

*"WO. ~ WO, I don't want no trouble with you young lady."*

The man quickly yelled, ducking fast behind the large tree.

*"What do you want?"*

Was the only thing Christina's terrified mind could come up with to say; as she kept a dead aim at the tree that the man was hiding behind.

*"Well, for starters, I would like to retrieve my turkey."*

The man said with a slight chuckle, still keeping himself safe behind the tree.

*"Who are you and where in the hell did you come from?"*

Christina demanded with a shaky voice, still keeping her aim at the tree.

*"What a potty mouth on such a pretty little girl; my name is Steve, and my house and family is a few miles from here."*

Steve explained from the protection of the large tree.

*"You have a family?"*

Christina asked, with a bit of relief in her voice as she lowered her bow.

*"Yes, Yes I do."*

Steve said, peeking his head out from behind the tree, and then raised his hand and gave a little friendly wave.

*"How do I know I can trust you?"*

Christina asked, remembering what Jim had said, {NEVER TRUST ANYONE.}

*"Well, I can show you some pictures."*

Steve answers, stepping out from behind his protection to show his trust in her.

Steve is a forty five year old man; five ft. nine in. tall; short brown hair and brown eyes; with a clean shaved face.

*"Just stay where you are until I get my turkey."*

Christina said, slowly walking backward in the direction of her turkey, and then she whistled for BLACKWALL to come.

*"There is a bad storm coming tonight, you are welcome to come and have dinner with me and my family."*

Steve said, watching the young girl mount a massive pile of black muscles.

"No thanks, I'll be fine."

Christina said with her turkey in hand, as she leans forward in the saddle, putting BLACKWALL into a forward motion.

Christina traveled only a short distance when she decides to stop and sets camp. She began to try to gather-up some firewood so she could cook her prize for dinner, but the snow was really starting to come down hard, and with no shelter a fire was imposable.

"Screw this."

Christina concludes, putting her turkey into a pouch and tied it up onto a limb, so to keep the varmints of the night from taking her prize, and then she climbed into her tent for the night.

# [MOM RETURNS]

Tonight Christina's dreams she is standing in the center of a field; the snow is coming down so hard see can't see more than a few feet in front of herself. She slowly turns in a circle, trying to see.

*"I told you to find shelter; why won't you listen to you mother?"*

Christina hears her mom's voice. She spins around until she spies a faded figure of her mom standing in the falling snow.

*"I'm trying mom."*

Christina explains, as she tried to move toward her mom, but found that she was frozen in place.

*"God will send people into your life to help you; you must learn to recognize these people."*

Christina's mom told her as she faded back into the snowy back ground.

*"WAIT MOM!! WAIT!"*

Christina shouted, trying with all her might to move in her direction.

Christina woke-up screaming, "wait.". She lay still for a few minutes wondering how much longer until day-break. She slowly slipped her arms out of the sleeping-bag and opened the front of her tent.

*"SHIT!! SHIT!! SHIT!!"*

Christina shouts in a whisper, noticing that her tent was buried under a pile of snow and day-light had already arrived.

The snow was still falling hard as Christina packed camp onto the back of BLACKWALL, then she pulled her frozen turkey from the limb as she rode out of the camp, turning BLACKWALL back toward the direction where she had met Steve, as her mother's words echoed through her head.

*"I think we are getting close my friend."*

Christina told BLACKWALL, noticing the aroma of smoke from a fire-place filling the air.

As the distance that separated Christina from Steve's farm house drew shorter, she began to hear the sound of people singing holiday songs. The house suddenly went silent, when she brought BLACKWALL to a halt in front of the porch.

*"Well potty mouth, I'm glad to see that you changed your mind."*

Steve said, stepping out the front door and onto the porch, still slipping into his coat.

*"My name is Christina, and yes sir; I do need shelter."*

Christina admitted, watching as a much younger version of Steve stepped out of the house, and stood beside Steve.

*"O'K. Christina, this is my son JR. he will show you to the barn. It looks like we have a winter guest."*

Steve said, giving the twenty year old looking man a hard slap on the back.

As Christina dismounted BLACKWALL, she handed Steve her solid frozen turkey and then shrugged her shoulders with a smile. Christina noticed a very pretty twenty year old red headed woman with very long hair, and a woman that looked to be Steve's age staring out the window and waving with big smiles. Christina smiled and waved back as she noticed the young red-head was holding a small infant.

With the horses put away, Christina and JR. quickly returned to the house just as the snow storm became white-out conditions.

Christina is welcomed into the fold with caring hugs from the two women as she enters through the front door. The large fire in the fireplace has the three room cabin nice and toasty. The aroma of roasting turkey and baking bread fills the air.

"*Christina; my name is Alice.*"

The twenty year old red-head woman said, pulling Christina into a tight embrace.

Christina gave Alice a warm smile as she pulled away, noticing that Alice was the same height as she is, maybe a smigen taller.

"*My name is Lesley.*"

The older woman said, as she reached and pulled Christina into another welcoming embrace; Christina could easily see over the top of this five ft. four in. woman.

Alice lovingly took Christina by the hand and firmly led her into the room at one side of the cabin. Alice began to shuffle through her neatly stack of folded clothes as Christina stood and watched.

"I'm Sorry Christina but you really, really stink; follow me."

Alice said with passion in her eyes, walking toward the door with an arm full of clean clothes.

Christina shyly followed Alice with her arm load of clean clothes back through the main room where she knew everyone could smell her, and into a tiny room attached to the back of the house. The room housed a large wash-tub with plenty of warm water that had been prepared for the occasion.

"O.K., get undressed and get in the tub; I'll wash your back, and then you can do the rest."

Alice said, putting the stack of clean clothes onto a shelf.

"Wait. You want me to get necked with you in here?"

Christina asked, with big eyes and a slight squeak in her voice.

"Yes. You are family now; I have the same thing as you, and I'm married with a new born; now stop being silly and get your ass in the tub."

Alice said, expressing authority in her voice, staring at Christina's eyes with her arms crossed over her chest.

Christina began to undress with a beet-red face, and then she slowly slipped into the tub and eased down into the warm water with her eyes closed, enjoying the warm experience.

"O.K. ~. So JR. is your husband."

Christina shyly said, trying to cover her young skinny, but well developed body with her small hands.

"Yes, and he is the best; and our baby's name is Steve the third."

Alice explained, taking a wash-cloth and a bar of soap, and then she began scrubbing Christina's back.

"So all the boy's are named Steve."

Christina said with a giggle, as she began to relax and enjoy her back rub.

"Yes; Steve Sr.; Steve Jr. and Steve the third. Now all done, you can do the rest."

Alice said with a giggle of her own, than she stood and started out of the room.

"Thank you."

Christina quickly said, watching Alice move the curtain that made the door.

"You're welcome sis."

Alice responded, disappearing through the certain.

Christina began to hear the house fill with the family singing familiar holiday songs. She got a big smile on her face and then she began to sing along as she enjoyed her warm bath. After many songs had been sung, the water in the tub and the air in the room had started to get a slight chilly. Christina quickly dried off, got dressed, and then joined the family around the fireplace.

"How old are you sis?"

Alice asked, reaching and gently taking Christina by the hand with a warm smile.

"Sixteen; no wait, what day is this?"

Christina asked, looking into Alice's deep green eyes.

"It's thanksgiving day babe."

Alice answers Christina, still waiting for the answer to her question.

"In that case, I'm seventeen."

Christina proudly said, sitting up a little bit taller.

"Well, I guess that we are going to have a double celebration; now let's go eat."

Lesley said, pulling Steve Sr. to his feet and starting for the kitchen.

The table was amazing, filled with everything that a thanksgiving dinner would have for a king. With everyone gathered around the kitchen table, tears began to run down Christina's cheeks; Alice started singing happy birthday to Christina, and the rest of the family joined in.

Through-out the rest of the cold winter Christina came to care and love her new family, especially her new sister Alice. She had marked the spot in her Atlas so to make sure she could find the way back to this place, knowing she would be returning back to her quest to find Sera as soon as spring arrives. For now Christina was happy she found a home and loving family for the holidays.

# MISSING YOU
### BY- RAYDON COOLEY

I'M TRAVELING DOWN.
LOST HIGHWAYS.
I'M HOPING THEY.
WILL LEAD ME YOUR WAY.
I'M SEARCHING FOR YOU.
I'M MISSING YOU.
ONCE AGAIN.
I SLEEP ALONE.
WITH NO PLACE.
I CAN CALL MY HOME.
I'M THINKING OF YOU.
I'M MISSING YOU.
I'M TRAVELING DOWN.
LOST HIGHWAYS.
I'M HOPING THEY.
WILL LEAD ME YOUR WAY.
I'M SEARCHING FOR YOU.
I'M MISSING YOU.

# CHAPTER FIVE
## WASHINGTON

Christina had spent the winter in the south-east part of Oregon with her second new family that had taken her in through the winter holidays, and had celebrated her seventeenth birthday with her. Now that spring has sprung, Christina resumed with her journey to find her older sister Sera. As she and her horse BLACKWALL make their way up to Seattle Washington, the weather is beginning to warm a bit on this day in late March, much warmer than it was when she started out at the beginning of the month. Seattle Washington is where her dad had told her the New U.S. Police had taken her older sister Sera, the last thing that her father had said to Christina was; *"go and find your sister."* words that she took to heart.

Christina had been camping on top of a hill- side for the last two days, watching a small farm through her binoculars down below.

*"I haven't seen anything move at the farm house for the last two days."*

Christina told BLACKWALL, climbing down from the tree with her binoculars in hand.

Christina sticks her foot into the stirrup and mounts BLACKWALL, than she slowly heads for the farm house, continuously looking around for any sudden danger that might pop out at her. The quietness was eerie as Christina cautiously rode through the deserted farm. She shuddered at the sight of the skeletal remains that laid in the back yard, two that were clearly small children. She dismounts BLACKWALL and slowly walks into the house.

*"Damned U.N. bastard."*

Christina whispered, looking around at the ram-sacked house.

Christina walked out through the back door and cautiously starts to walk in the direction of the barn, with BLACKWALL tagging close behind. She carefully opens the barn door just enough for her and BLACKWALL to slip through. The two enter into the barn, BLACKWALL heads straight for a bag of oats lying open on the floor.

*"I hope those oats aren't fermented."*

Christina giggled at BLACKWALL, causing him to look up for just a moment, than he returned to his munchies.

Christina noticed the large tarp in the center of the barn that seemed to have been coated with some kind of silver coating that was covering up something big. She pulled the edge of tarp back to reveal the frontend of an older farm truck. She quickly pulls the tarp off and opened the squeaky door to see the keys waiting.

*"Damn-it-all-to-hell."*

Christina whispered, when she attempts to start the truck with a dead battery.

*"This is a big bag of shit."*

Christina said, with a phrase that she had heard Alice say many times; she exits the truck and then slams the truck door shut.

Christina begins to wonder all around in the barn as BLACKWALL continued eating his oats. She noticed a tiny room at the back of the barn; she opened the door to what looked to be a large closet. Her eyes grew big as she saw three new car batteries still wrapped in their original packaging sitting on a shelf. Christina quickly went to work changing out the battery in the truck. Being raised on a horse ranch is once again coming in handy. She jumps back into the truck and closes her eyes, raising her head up as if praying.

"Please; please; please."

Christina kept repeating, slowly turning the key to start the truck.

"YES!! YES!! **YES!!** Thank you sweet Jesus."

Christina shouts, bouncing up and down in the seat, as the truck began to spit and sputter, and then roars to life.

Christina quickly jumped from the truck and pushed the door to the barn open and then she pulled the truck out and backed it up to a single stall horse trailer. Christina looked down at the fuel-gage to see that it showed the truck has a full tank of gas.

"You better not be lying to me."

Christina told the animate object.

Christina found a pair of gloves tucked into the side pocket of the driver door of the truck, and then she headed to hook up the trailer.

BLACKWALL had a bit of a stagger in his step from eating the fermented oats, as Christina loads him into the trailer.

"Seattle by morning."

Christina said with a big smile, pulling out onto the highway in her new older truck.

Christina began to sing familiar songs that she could remembered from her C.D.'s, as she drove down the road with the window down and a cool breeze blowing through the truck. She would give out a "Thank you" every time she crossed over a bridge and saw the ragging water below, flowing from the melting snow. Christina stuck to the back roads so to avoid the cities. The sun was sinking low in the west when Christina came across a bridge that had been washed away. She was now getting a lesson on backing up a trailer. The closes drive where she could turn around was one mile back, but after one hour she was there and back in a forward direction. She only had to backtrack twice due to bridges that had collapsed. After driving all night and into the morning on deserted roads, Christina was just fifty miles from Seattle Washington when the old truck began to sputter and then ran out of gas.

*"Shit, shit, shit."*

Christina said, as she coasted to a stop in the center of the road.

Christina exited the old truck and slowly walked to the back of the horse trailer as she pulled the gloves over her hands. After she had BLACKWALL unloaded and saddled she began to pack her gear onto his back.

*"We got to go my friend."*

Christina whispers, catching the subtle aroma of camp fire smoke in the air as she mounted BLACKWALL.

*"What's your hurry?"*

A man's voice said loudly, from the tree line alone the side of the road.

Christina spun around in the saddle and seen a small man that looked to be at least one-hundred years old with long wiry gray hair with a beard to match, and his clothes didn't look much better.

*"Who are you?"*

Christina asked in a demanding voice, as she sat on BLACKWALL, ready to run.

*"They call me Lucky; that is they use to call me Lucky, before the dirty bomb destroyed Seattle."*

Lucky said, standing just outside the edge of the trees.

*"What do you mean destroyed?"*

Christina asked, with clear authority in her voice.

*"Has anyone ever told you that you have a sexy butt?"*

Lucky asks Christina point-blank, giving her a toothless smile.

*"I don't like that."*

Christina answered point-blank, as she gave Lucky a hard stare.

*"What, you don't like that you have a sexy butt?"*

Lucky said; breaking into a laugh and a hard cough, both at the same time.

Lucky's body began to tremble and then he slowly started sinking to the ground.

*"This is a big bag of shit."*

Christina whispered, leaning forward in the saddle and moving toward the old man.

The old man had sunk down onto his hands and knees, coughing as if one of his lunges could come up at any time.

Christina dismounts with her canteen in her hand, then squatted down to help Lucky to sturdy himself into a sitting position and then leaned him up against a small tree. Christina held the canteen sturdy as the old man took a sip with shaky hands. Lucky leaned back up against the tree, closing his eyes and taking in a few deep breaths.

*"Are you O.K.?"*

Christina asked, slowly sitting down on the ground in front of Lucky, slowly scanning his shriveled and wrinkled face.

*"I haven't laughed that hard in a long time; yea, I'm fine sexy butt."*

Lucky said, his breathing returned to normal as he gave Christina a toothless smile.

*"O.K. Grandpa, my name is Christina; call me Christina."*

Christina demanded, handing the canteen back to Lucky.

Lucky took himself a long drink and then smiled at Christina.

*"No, no; I'm going to call you sexy butt."*

Lucky said with a big chuckle, as he slowly handing Christina her canteen back.

*"O.K. Grandpa, you have laughed enough for one day; now where do you live?"*

Christina asked with a giggle, knowing this old man did not have enough stamina or strength to attempt anything.

*"Over there behind those thick bushes."*

Lucky answered, pointing over toward the bushes about fifty feet away.

"O.K. Grandpa, let's get you home."

Christina said, pulling the small mans arm around her shoulder and helping him to his feet.

Christina helped Lucky into his camp with BLACKWALL right behind. She laid him down on an army cot that was raised on one end. She looks around the small camp to see a stack of half rusted unopened food cans with no labels, sitting beside a small tent. She was glad to see the small running stream a few feet behind the camp. After Christina had unpacked BLACKWALL and sat her tent, she retrieved a bag of dry beans that Debby had given her and began the chore of building a fire and cooking the beans.

"Why are you here?"

Lucky asked, watching as Christina happily whistling a tune while making a pot of beans.

"I'm looking for my sister."

Christina answered, glancing up at Lucky with a caring smile.

Christina poured the beans into the pot of hot water with a bit of seasoning that Debby had given her.

*"O.K.; but that's not what I meant. Why did you stay here with me? Anyone else would have just kept going on their way."*

Lucky said, slowly raising himself up into a sitting position.

*"That's not how I was raised, that's not who I am."*

Christina said, with her mother's face in her mind, and her words; "NEVER FORGET WHO YOU ARE"; echoing through her head.

*"Now tell me about Seattle."*

Christina said, taking a seat on the cot next to Lucky and wrapping her arm around his shoulder and giving him a caring embrace.

Lucky began to tell a horror story about U.N DEMON'S, and how they took over the city. They had fought the New U.S Police about a year ago, and then someone set off a small suitcase bomb that covered the down town part of Seattle with radiation.

*"My sister was a U.S. Police; do you know what happened to them?"*

Christina asked with a slight shake in her voice, fearing what she might hear from Lucky.

*"The ones that came from other places had already left, going back to where they had come from."*

Lucky answered, putting a hand on Christina's shoulder and giving a slight squeeze.

*"O.K. so I have to go to Pennsylvania."*

Christina whispered, starring forward as if she were in a trance.

*"Yes, you can't stay here for very long sexy butt."*

Lucky said, with a tear slowly rolling down his cheek.

*"I can't leave you here alone."*

Christina quickly said, gently taking a holt of Lucky's hand.

*"Yes, you have to leave; I am dying from all the radiation, and if you stay you will get sick just like me; now tomorrow you will leave and go find your sister."*

Lucky demanded with a quivering voice, as Christina pulled him into a tight hug with tears running down her cheeks.

After dinner Christina said good-night and settled into her sleeping bag. Christina lay awake in her screen tent as her mother's voice came to her once again; "GOD WILL

SEND PEOPLE INTO YOUR LIFE TO HELP YOU."

"I miss you so much mom."

Christina whispered, as she faded off into a deep sleep.

## {WARNING DREAM}
### TONIGHT CHRISTINA DREAMS OF HER MOTHER.

Christina was sitting by the camp- fire when she heard her mom's soft voice.

*"Christina I am proud of you."*

Mom said in her soft voice.

Christina jumped to her feet and then she began turning in a circle until she spied her mother standing a few feet away, with Lucky standing beside her with his toothless smile.

*"I will never forget who I am, I promise."*

Christina said, being just a little bit confused as to why Lucky would be standing beside her mom.

*"Listen to me sweetheart, there is coming a time when you will have to kill."*

Mom said, with authority in her voice.

*"NO!! NO!! I will never kill anyone; that's not who I am."*

Christina demanded loudly, with her body beginning to tremble.

*"I understand; there will be someone sent to you; now I'm*

*going to taking Lucky home, I love you sweetheart."*

Mom said, as she and Lucky both began to fade away into a fog.

*"Good-by mom, I love you."*

Christina softly whispers, as tears streamed down her face.

Christina woke-up with tears running down her cheeks. She slowly set up and turned to look over at Lucky through her screen tent. It was clear to see he was no longer breathing.

*"Thanks mom."*

Christina whispered, as she covered-up Lucky with his blanket, then she packed BLACKWALL and started for Pennsylvania.

# CHAPTER SIX
## NEW COMPANION

Christina decided that she would take highway [2] that runs most of the way across the country at the border of Canada. It would give her easy passage with crossing the high mountains that she would have to travail over, and bridges to cross ravaging rivers that would be swollen from the melting snow. It's a back highway with mostly small towns, a safe pathway to take Christina thought.

*"I miss our old truck."*

Christina said to BLACKWALL, as they made their way through the mountainous terrain.

It's been three weeks since she left Seattle and Christina was now on highway [2] heading east toward Pennsylvania. As the sun began to sink low into the west and knowing that the nights are still getting extremely cold this time of year, Christina guides BLACKWALL into the tree-line to set camp for the night. She climbed up a tree with her binoculars to scout the aria. like she done several times a day to see if the person that her mom said she would send to her was anywhere in sight.

"*Nooo; no, no, no.*"

Christina whispers to herself, holding her binoculars as sturdy as she could.

Christina saw four large men dressed in U.N. uniforms riding horses in her direction, following her exact tracks.

"*Shit, shit, shit.*"

Christina continuously repeated, as she quickly climbing down the tree.

"*We got to go; we got to go.*"

Christina repeated, with fear prevalent in her voice.

Christina mounted BLACKWALL and put him into a fast trot through the woods. As the sun disappears below the horizon and as darkness defeated the light, Christina exited the woods and put BLACKWALL into a slightly faster run down the shoulder of the highway. Tears had began to roll down her cheeks as her mother's words; "YOU WILL HAVE TO KILL."; kept running through her head. Christina was glad that the moon was full and shinning bright. When she had reached the crest of a long slopping hill she pulled BLACKWALL to a halt and looked back down the road through her binoculars.

*"This is a gigantic bag of shit."*

Christina whispered through her tears, seeing the four men following her tracks.

*"Go, go, go!"*

Christina shouted out nervously, as she put BLACKWALL into a hard run.

BLACKWALL could since the fear that was resonating from Christina's body, as he put large chunks of real-estate behind them. The rest of the night BLACKWALL would run for a while and then slow to a fast walk.

As the morning sun began to peek above the horizon, Christina set on top of another hill and looks back through her binoculars, she could feel BLACKWALL'S deep heavy breathing.

*"Damn-it BLACKWALL, their gaining on us."*

Christina said, than she turned her attention up the road in the direction they were heading.

Christina spies an abandon gas station a short distance away. Being inexperienced with her situation, she heads BLACKWALL for the deserted building at a fast trot. When she reaches the station she quickly dismounts and pushes the front door open and then pulled BLACKWALL through the door, she headed for the opened walk-in refrigerator. As Christina sank to the floor in the back of the refrigerator she began to cry and tremble with fear. She realized that she was now trapped. BLACKWALL put himself between her and the door.

*"jhrdb mng hkjeu gsotm."*

Is what Christina heard as the four men entered through the front door.

Christina refused to let herself pass-out as she trembled uncontrollably. She screamed loudly when a large ugly fat face with cheeks that hung halfway down his neck pressed up against the glass door that a costumer would have use back in the day.

*"djft bsdeij nb jwrbo bsrk oykrma."*

Is what Christina heard the man say, as he gave her a snaggled-tooth smile through the glass door.

Christina became terrified when the door handle to the refrigerator began to jiggle, all she could think of to do was pick up empty bottles and throw them at the door. Instantly her ears begin to reverberate with a thunderous sound echoing throughout the building. The door handle went still as the ugly man turned toward the front of the store with a look of shock on his face. Another thunder echoed throughout the building as the fat ugly man with saggy cheeks instantly dropped to the floor with blood squirting from his head. All Christina could do was sit still and stare as the other two men ran through the store and out the back. Christina set frozen as the door handle began to jiggle once again. When the door swung open she saw a tall older slender woman with long coal black hair and big brown eyes standing in the doorway, with a huge hand-gun in her hand. Christina began to giggle as the world started spinning, and then everything went black.

*"Easy boy, easy."*

The dark haired lady told BLACKWALL as she slowly moved around him.

The dark haired woman reached down and picked up the skinny teenage girl into her arms and carried her out of the store as BLACKWALL followed close behind.

Christina began to regain conciseness, looking up as her eyes began to slowly open, she saw new sprouts on the large tree limbs above her. She ran her hand over the soft blanket that she was lying on as she looked around, realizing she was laying on top of a soft sleeping-bag in the shade up-under a huge tree.

"About damned time."

The dark haired woman exclaimed, with a raspy but sexy voice.

The woman's voice startled Christina into a sitting position.

"Who the hell are you?"

Christina softly said, with prominent fear in her voice as she stared at the woman with her eyes opened wide.

"Who the hell are you, and what the hell were you thinking? That had to be the most ignorant thing I have ever seen anyone do."

The woman proclaimed, and then took a long draw from her small corn-cob pipe and slowly exhaled.

"My name is Christina."

Christina chocked out, as the stench of the smoke filled the air.

"Rosie."

Rosie said point blank, holding the pipe out toward Christina.

"No thanks, I don't smoke."

Christina said, sitting up in an Indian stance.

"Take a drag or I will shove it down your puny little throat."

Rosie said with authority, staring straight into Christina's eyes as she held the pipe out in her direction.

Christina slowly reached and took the pipe from Rosie with one hand and held her nose with the other, then reluctantly lifted the pipe to her lips.

"*Big drag, and inhale.*"

Rosie demanded loudly, staring straight into Christina's eyes.

Christina fell to one elbow and began to cough as if she were Lucky, dropping the pipe to the ground. Rosie picked up the pipe with a giggle and took another long drag and then waited for Christina to catch her breath.

"*What is that shit?*"

Christina asked, as the world began to spin, and a deep warmth surged through her body.

"*Marijuana.*"

Rosie said, as if Christina should know.

"*Are you trying to kill me?*"

Christina shouted, falling back on the soft sleeping-bag as she felt her body going numb.

"*No sweetheart, but you will sleep sound for awhile longer.*"

Rosie giggled, taking another huge drag as she watched Christina fade off into a deep sleep.

Rosie is a Native American; forty six years old; six foot tall; one-hundred sixty lb.'s of pure muscle; with unusually soft smooth skin and large brown eyes on her beautiful face.

With Christina in a sound sleep and the U.N. DEMON'S on the run, Rosie retrieves her bow-and-arrow and then heads into the woods to collect something for dinner.

As Christina's eyes began to open, her mouth is so dry that she can't even swallow. She pushes herself up and stumbles over to BLACKWALL and pulls her canteen from the saddle and chugs down the tasty water. She walked back over to the sleeping-bag and takes a seat.

*"I don't like this."*

Christina whispered, unable to get her brain to function correctly.

Christina begins to recollect her slim escape. As she looks around the camp she noticed a large solid white horse standing across the camp.

*"Rosie."*

Christina whispers, forcing her fuzzy brain to function.

Christina hears a noise coming through the woods behind her. She turns to see a beautiful tall woman with long black hair, carrying the hind quarter of a deer across her shoulder. Christina watched as Rosie carried the meat into camp and plopped it down beside the fire pit.

"Your awake; why haven't you built a fire?"

Rosie asked, with a demanding tone in her voice as she stared at Christina.

"I'm not thinking straight; I don't like that you forced me to do drugs."

Christina whispered in a challenging tone, looking down at the ground.

"I did not force you to do anything."

Rosie explained, as she puts some starter twigs into the fire pit.

"Yes you did, you threatened me."

Christina countered, looking up at Rosie.

"Yea I did, but I did not force you; you must learn to take a stand for yourself."

Rosie said, striking her flint so to start up the fire in the pit.

"Mom sent you to me."

Christina softly said, taking in every inch of the tall woman.

"What the hell are you talking about?"

Rosie quickly asked, freezing into place and staring into Christina's eyes.

"In a dream; my mom said she would send someone to help me."

Christina nervously said, hopping that Rosie wouldn't think she was eccentric.

"Well I'll be damned, a child dreamer."

Rosie said, rising up and then walking over and sitting down beside Christina.

"So you don't think I'm crazy?"

Christina asked, looking down at the ground.

"No, no sweetheart, I believe you have a special gift; now as long as we are travailing together I want to hear every dream you have."

Rosie explained, putting one of her arms around Christina and pulling her into an embrace.

"Where did you come from?"

Christina asked, leaning into Rosie's warm embrace.

"I'm from up-state New York."

Rosie said, leaning her head down on top of Christina's head.

"*No. I mean when you found me at the store.*"

Christina corrected, enjoying having the new friend that she could talk with.

"*Oh. Well, I started following you from the old man's camp.*"

Rosie said, rocking Christina side to side, enjoying having a child to care for.

"*WAIT!! You knew Lucky?*"

Christina said with a squeak in her voice, quickly raising up and looking into Rosie's big brown eyes.

"*No babe, I came upon you the morning you left the camp.*"

Rosie said with a warm smile, looking down into Christina's deep blue eyes.

"*So are you like me, do you take care of people that need help.*"

Christina said, as she slowly returned her head back into Rosie's bosom.

"*Well not exactly like you, I mean, I would never hide in a room with only one way in and one way out.*"

Rosie said with a slight giggle, returning to rocking Christina.

*"Yea, that was kind of dumb; so why are you in Washington?"*

Christina asked with her eyes closed, as she began to get into the rhythm of Rosie's rocking.

*"About three years ago the government sent me to Port Angles, now I'm on my way home, upstate New York."*

Rosie said, as a bit of anger seeped into her voice.

*"WAIT!! WAIT!! You are a U.S Police?"*

Christina shouts out, quickly sitting up straight and taking Rosie's arm into a tight grip.

*"Yes, Yes I was, until about a year ago."*

Rosie said with curiosity written on her face.

*"Did you know Sera?"*

Christina asked, with a raised voice and big eyes.

*"Yes, I knew a young girl named Sera."*

Rosie said, gently placing her hand on Christina's cheek, realizing that she was Sera's sister.

"Do you know where she is?"

Christina asked, quickly standing up and looked down at Rosie.

"No. She said she had to go and find her family."

Rosie answered, reaching out and taking Christina's hand, pulling her back down to her seat.

"I have to go to Pennsylvania."

Christina said, staring out into space as if she were in a trance.

"Hay ~ hay; settle down babe, we will go to Pennsylvania together; now slow down and let's start dinner."

Rosie said, pulling the teenager into her embrace.

"Yea, your right."

Christina agreed, squeezing Rosie as tight as she could.

After dinner they sat around the camp fire and took turns singing their favorite songs. Rosie would chant her most favorite ancestor's Native American songs, and Christina would sing the most resent songs she could remember hearing on the radio, before all the electricity went out. When the mosquitoes began their assault on the two girls they said good-night and retired into their tents.

## CHRISTINA'S DREAM
### [A MESSAGE FOR A FRIEND]

Christina's dream starts out with her and her mom standing on a front porch of a small cabin on the side of a mountain. A young woman was in the front yard playing with a small child. The woman looked to be in her early twenties, clearly a Native American with her long hair up in pony-tails. The child looked to be around three years old.

*"I want you to mind Rosie; she is a very smart and important woman."*

Christina's mom said as they watched the two playing in the yard.

*"I promise mom; I miss you a whole bunch."*

Christina said, as she wrapped her arm around her mom's waist; now being able to tell when she was dreaming.

*"I have to go for now; remember to listen to Rosie."*

Christina's mom said, as she took Christina into a tight embrace.

*"I will mom."*

Christina agreed, with her dream beginning to fade.

Christina woke-up with a pleasing smile on her face, as the sun was peeking over the horizon. She quickly got dressed and then went to prepare breakfast. She was hoping to have breakfast done and ready before her proverbial protector woke up. She started the fire and then quickly retrieved the pancake mix that she gathered along the way, and began to make pancakes.

Rosie had a big smile on her face and a corn cob pipe sticking out of her mouth as she exited her tent and smiled over toward Christina.

*"You got to be kidding me, how can you even think when you're smoking that shit so early?"*

Christina demanded, shaking her head and returning back to her chore of making pancakes.

*"I can't think without it babe; I think I do need to go pee."*

Rosie said, as she inhaled a deep breath of smoke and started toward a spot out of camp.

*"Where do you even get that crap?"*

Christina yelled behind Rosie, finishing up the pancakes, and going to retrieve the last jar of honey from her saddlebag.

*"It's a damned weed sweetheart, it grows wild in the woods."*

Rosie yelled back at Christina, from her squatting position; enjoying the feeling of relief from her bladder.

"WAIT! Are you saying you just pick it from the woods?"

Christina asked, as if she thought that was completely imposable.

"Yes babe, after breakfast I'll show you."

Rosie said, fastening her pants as she walked back into camp.

Rosie pulled her canteen from its place and rinsed her hands, watching Christina finishing with her pancakes.

"O.K but I need to tell you about my dream first."

Christina said, pouring honey over the top of Rosie's pancakes.

Christina and Rosie were quietly eating their pancakes when Christina began to tell Rosie about her dream. She explained that in her dream Rosie was in her twenties and she had a three year old little girl. Rosie slowly set down her plate and stared at Christina for a moment.

"Christina, if you are a true dreamer you do not dream of things from the past; you will only dream of the present or the future."

Rosie said, taking Christina's plate and sitting it down, and then took a hold of her hands tightly.

"*So what you are saying is that the woman and child are at the cabin now.*"

Christina said with amassment, staring into Rosie's eyes.

"*Yes, now listen to me O.K; close your eyes and concentrate; look at the woman and tell me what you see.*"

Rosie said, with a shaky voice and water filled eyes.

This was the first time Christina had seen a tiny crack in Rosie's sturdy shield. Rosie looked into Christina's eyes as a tear slowly drifted down her cheek.

"*O.K.; O.K.*"

Christina softly whispered, tightening her grip on Rosie's hands as she closed her eyes.

"*I see her; she looks like you just younger; she is playing with the little child in the front yard of the cabin up in the mountains.*"

Christina said, as she began to relax, and enjoy her new found ability.

"*O.K. Christina, look at her hair; does she have anything in her hair?*"

Rosie asked in a calm voice, as tears ran down her cheeks.

*"Her hair is in ponytails; Yes, yes, she has like silvery tie thingy's holding her long ponytails together, **SHIT!!***

Christina shouts, pulling her hands away from Rosie's and quickly opening her eyes.

*"WHAT! What did you see sweetheart?"*

Rosie asked, gently taking Christina's hands again and staring into her blue eyes.

*"She saw me; my god Rosie, she saw me."*

Christina said with a trembling voice, as she quickly pulled Rosie into her embrace.

Rosie and Christina set holding eachother in a tight embrace for a moment, both trembling with tears running down their faces. Rosie took a deep shaky breath and began to speak.

*"It's O.K. babe, you were just remembering your dream; she did not see you."*

Rosie quietly whispered, gently rubbing Christina's hair down her back.

Christina quickly leaned back so that she could see into Rosie's big brown eyes.

*"No Rosie, it wasn't the same as my dream, it was different, she had different clothes on; it wasn't my dream; how could she see*

*me Rosie? She looked straight at me with a shocked look on her face; she saw me Rosie, she saw me."*

Christina explained through her tears, and then fell back into Rosie's arms.

Rosie set holding the crying teenager and gently rocked back and forth, considering what Christina had said. Rosie reached into her pocket and pulled out her corn-cob pipe.

*"NO!! Hell no; I need you to talk to me!"*

Christina demanded, grabbing the pipe from Rosie and throwing it across the camp.

Rosie sat with a look of shock on her face as she stared at Christina, and then she turned and looked at her pipe lying on the ground across the camp. She turned back to Christina and began to speak softly.

*"Christina sweetheart, have you ever known someone who took medicine from a doctor to keep their nerves calm, and without the medicine they could not function?"*

Rosie asked in a soft calm voice, staring into Christina's eyes.

*"Yea, back before everything went crazy, I knew a few people like that."*

Christina whispered, slightly tilting her head and giving Rosie a curious look.

*"Well babe, there are no more doctor's; the pipe is my medicine."*

Rosie explained to Christina, with tears still rolling down her cheeks.

Christina slowly rose up and walked across the camp. She retrieved the pipe and gently returned it to Rosie.

*"I'm so sorry Rosie, I didn't know."*

Christina softly said, handing the pipe back to Rosie.

*"Let's go and find you some medicine."*

Christina said, taking Rosie by the hand and starting down a deer trail through the woods.

Rosie began to pull Christina to a stop as they walked through the woods, showing her different plants and berries. Each time Rosie would take the time to explain all of the healing powers of each plant. Christina meticulously paid very close attention, remembering her mother's words; "Listen to Rosie." as she took mental picture of each plant.

*"O.K. Stop Rosie; I smell a skunk."*

Christina said, taking Rosie by the arm and pulling her to a stop as she sniffed the air.

*"Yes; Which way?"*

Rosie quickly asked, she too had begun to sniff the air.

*"That way"*

Christina whispered, pointing in a particular direction, after tuning in a circle and sniffing the air.

*"Perfect."*

Rosie said with excitement in her voice.

Rosie began moving into the direction that Christina was pointing.

*"Where in the hell are you going?"*

Christina whispered loudly, following as Rosie started through the woods.

*"Marijuana."*

Rosie said with a smile, walking up to a tall thick bush,

She began to break off the thick tops of the plant and stuff them into the saddle bag she had brought along with them.

*"Wait! Are you saying marijuana smells like a stinky skunk?"*

Christina asked in amassment, as she began helping Rosie pick the tops off of the *weed.*

*"Yes dear, the good stuff does."*

Rosie answered, concentrating on her chore with a smile, offering her pipe to Christina.

"*No. No thank you, my nerves are just fine.*"

Christina said with a slight giggle in her voice, moving up wind of the smoke.

"*O.K. Let's go break camp and be on our way.*"

Rosie said, with her saddle-bag so full that the top would not close.

# CHAPTER SEVEN
## LESSONS TO LEARN

Over the next two years Christina and Rosie became very close to each-other, as they travailed across the country surviving. Christina found that Rosie was not quite as hard-ass as she liked to pretend to be. Rosie continued to teach Christina how to identify different types of plants and how to mix them together and use them for different ailments. Rosie also taught Christina all about her dream powers and how to use them, but Christina refused to use her new found out-of-body powers; it just scared her too much. She was afraid that another spirit might take over her body.

Christina and Rosie rode into Christina's families horse ranch in Pennsylvania in late fall, tears were streamed down Christina's face and her breathing became very jagged. Everything was gone, burnt to the ground. The only thing left standing was the small sagging hay barn.

"Do you think Sera was here?"

Christina asks Rosie through her tears, as they rode through the snow toward the hay barn.

*"I don't know sweetheart, let's set up camp in the barn and tonight we will meditate and try to have a dream that will let us know."*

Rosie suggested, realizing the pain that Christina was in as they slowly approached the small hay barn.

Christina and Rosie unsaddled their horses in silence. Christina would stop every couple of minutes and look out the barn door and began to sob. Slowly camp was set and the horses were put into the stall where hay was plentiful. As the light began to dim inside the barn, Christina and Rosie sat on a sleeping bag. Rosie filled her corn-cob pipe and used one of her hundred of lighters that she had gathered up every time they passed through a small town.

*"I think I need some medicine."*

Christina said with a squeaky voice that was becoming hoarse from all her constant crying.

*"Are you sure babe?"*

Rosie asked, with a surprised look and surprise in her voice as Christina reached for her pipe.

Rosie watched as Christina held her nose with one hand and lifted the pipe to her lips with the other. Christina took a tiny drag from the pipe and inhaled. She coughed a few seconds and then took another drag, a little bit bigger than the last. She coughed a bit more. Then she took a large drag and inhaled, trying her best to hold it in like she had seen Rosie doing it. Christina began to cough hard as she held the pipe up in the air for Rosie to take from her. As Rosie took the pipe Christina collapsed across the sleeping bag with her head landing in Rosie's lap.

*"Are you O.K. babe?"*

Rosie asked, exhaling her big puff of smoke, as she pushed Christina's hair from her face.

*"Yea. Today is my birthday. I'm nineteen today."*

Christina answered, taking Rosie's hand in her own and fading off to sleep.

*"I'm sorry that I forgot."*

Rosie whispered, lying down beside Christina and pulling another sleeping bag over them, and then cuddled her up into her arms for the night.

# [SPECIAL DREAM]

In Christina's dream tonight she and Rosie are sitting on the front porch of the cabin up in the mountains. They watch as Rosie's daughter and her granddaughter play out in the yard. Christina's mom came out of the door and took a seat beside her.

*"Christina sweetheart, you can stay and visit for a time, but you must keep looking for Sera."*

Mom explained to Christina, as she put her arm around Christina's shoulder.

*"So Sera's is O.K.?"*

Christina asked, leaning into her mom's warm embrace.

*"You must keep looking for Sera, I must go now."*

Mom said to Christina, as the dream began to fade.

Christina wakes with a smile on her face. She smells the odor of wood burning mixed in with the sweet aroma of food cooking. As Christina looks around the barn she can tell that the sun is shining today, but there is no Rosie. She rose and went to peek out the door. Rosie stood in front of a large bar-b-cue grill, cooking something.

*"What's cooking?"*

Christina asked, walking out of the barn and up beside Rosie.

*"Well good morning birthday girl. I was hoping to give you breakfast in bed; O well; I found where the chickens are laying all of their eggs, so we are having roasted chicken and fried eggs."*

Rosie said, as she lifted the top to the grill and turned over the chicken.

*"I talked to mom last-night; Sera is O.K."*

Christina excitedly said, gently leaning her head up against Rosie.

*"Wow, so you saw Sera?"*

Rosie asked, putting an arm around Christina's shoulder and pulling her close.

*"Well no, I did see your daughter, and mom told me that I had to keep looking for Sera; why would she tell me that if she is not O.K.?"*

Christina asked, with a little bit of aggravation in her voice.

*"Sweetheart, there are some things that we are not allowed to know, because if we did know, then it would alter the big plan."*

Rosie explained, raising the top of the grill and placing the pan of scrambled eggs onto the heat.

*"O.K. I'm going to go with you to your family's house and meet your daughter and then I have to go and look for Sera; I mean; I would not want to screw up the big plan."*

Christina said with a giggle, helping Rosie take breakfast off the grill.

"O.K. smart-ass, let's eat so we can get on our way before the big storms get here."

Rosie said, with her own giggle as she and Christina headed for the barn.

Christina and Rosie rode out of the horse ranch in silence with tears rolling down their cheeks. Christina could not bring herself to look back at her families devastated homestead.

After a week of hard fast riding, this day was overcast with a bit of a nip in the air. Rosie pulled SNOWFLAKE to a stop as she spun him around. Closing her eyes she looked up and took a deep breath and exhaled slowly.

"Christina; we are being followed."

Rosie said in a calm voice, lowering her eyes to meet Christina's.

"How do you know that, Rosie?"

Christina asked, with a slight squeak in her voice, giving Rosie a nervous look.

"Well babe, the same way that you have dreams; I was given a gift."

Rosie explained, giving Christina a warm and comforting smile.

"O.K. what are we going to do?"

Christina whispered, as if the person might be close enough to hear.

*"I want you to follow SNOWFLAKE, and she will lead you to a good hiding place. Wait there until I whistle."*

Rosie explained, as she looked for a low limb to grab onto.

*"NO!! You can't fight them all alone, I can't lose you Rosie."*

Christina demanded, as her body clearly began to tremble.

*"No, no sweetheart, there is only one, and who-ever this person is, doesn't have very much confidence; now do what I said."*

Rosie ordered, as she reached up and grabbed a hold of a low limb and quickly disappeared off the back of SNOWFLAKE. That caught Christina completely off guard. She began to laugh as she turned in the saddle and saw Rosie sitting on a limb up in the tall tree. She and the horses slowly rode away. Christina followed SNOWFLAKE a short distance down the trail, and then SNOWFLAKE quickly turned and went behind a group of tall, thick bushes, than she just stood still like she had done this many, many times before.

Christina was becoming impatient after sitting for thirty minutes and watching the white statue. Suddenly her ears perked up and she started back down the trail toward the direction that they had left Rosie sitting in a tree, BLACKWALL instantly began to follow. As Rosie came into Christina's view, Christina could see an Indian man in his early twenty's with long black hair, sitting and leaning back against a small tree with a bloody nose, and with Rosie standing in front of him. Rosie watched Christina and the two horses as they hurried down the trail toward her.

*"You have 'GOT' to teach me that trick."*

Christina exclaim, quickly dismounting and staring at the young long haired man that was holding his bloody nose.

*"I can do that; I caught myself a real live man."*

Rosie said, as if she was all excited, and then pointed at the man.

*"Yes, I can see that; so are you going to kill him now or later?"*

Christina asked as sincere as she possibly could; doing her best not to break a smile.

Christina and Rosie stood and stared at the young man as he held his nose between his thumb and fingers, to stop the bleeding. With eyes the size of small saucers, all he could do was sit and mumble uncontrollably and shake his head. Rosie turned toward Christina.

*"He is about your age, so I thought that you might like to keep him as a pet."*

Rosie said with a straight face, as she stared at Christina.

*"Why would I want a man that got his ass kicked by a woman?"*

Christina asked, turning her back toward the man, unable to control the smile on her face any longer.

*"Well shit, then I guess we'll just kill him now."*

Rosie said, reaching into her saddle bag and pulled out her colt 45.

Christina and Rosie broke into laughter as the man began to whine like a small puppy.

*"O shut up dumb-ass, we're not going to kill you; but I do want to know who you are and why you are following us."*

Rosie said with a giggle, putting her gun back into its place.

When Rosie and Christina turned back to question the man, they saw him passed out cold and laying flat on the ground.

"*Well shit!*"

Rosie exclaimed, in disbelief.

"*I concur.*"

Christina said, as she and Rosie broke out in laughter.

Rosie took the man's sleeping-bag from his horse and rolled the man into it, and then she zipped him up in it. Christina and Rosie began to set up camp for the night.

"*O.K. dumb-ass, get up and set your tent.*"

Christina said with a giggle, when she heard the man begin to moan.

"*My name is Stormy, so please call me Stormy.*"

Stormy said, sticking his head out of the sleeping-bag with dry blood across his face.

"*No, no I'm going to call you dumb-ass.*"

Christina said, looking over at Rosie with a big smile on her face.

Stormy pulled his tent from his horse and began to set it up. Then he retrieved his canteen and washed the dry blood from his face.

*"I'm a tracker, not a warrior"*

Stormy whispered, after he had his tent set.

*"What did you say?"*

Christina quickly enquired, instantly turning and looking at Stormy.

*"I'm not a warrior."*

Stormy said, taking his handkerchief from his back pocket and carefully drying his face.

*"NO! Before that."*

Christina demanded, taking a few steps toward Stormy.

*"I'm a tracker."*

Stormy said, holding his head high as he stared at Christina with his eyes beginning to turn black and blue.

*"Will you teach me how to track?"*

Christina asked, walking over to Stormy and gripping him by the arm.

*"Only if you promise me that your friend will not attack me again."*

Stormy said, looking over at Rosie with a hard look.

Rosie stood tall and gave Stormy and Christina a big smile.

*"I promise, all the ass whippings are over; right Rosie?"*

Christina insisted, turning and giving a pleading look toward Rosie.

*"As long as he can behave himself."*

Rosie countered, reaching into her vest pocket and retrieving her pipe.

Stormy gave Rosie a big smile and then he reached into his pocket and pulled out his own pipe.

*"Shit! I'm surrounded by druggies."*

Christina said, turning and starting for her tent, shaking her head as she heard Rosie and Stormy's laughter.

Christina was lying in her tent fading off to sleep, with the stench of marijuana filling up the air, and with the sounds of Rosie and their new found friend Stormy chanting their native songs, as they set around the camp fire.

# [CHRISTINA DREAMS]

Christina is once again sitting out on the front porch of the cabin with Rosie, watching the little girl playing in the yard. Christina noticed Rosie's daughter was sitting on the corner of the porch wrapped tightly in the arms of Stormy, completely content.

*"I am very proud of you Christina."*

Mom's voice softly said, coming from behind Christina.

Christina turned to see her mother sitting in the rocker on the porch.

*"I'm paying attention to what Rosie is teaching me mom."*

Christina said, as she stood and went to stand beside her mother.

*"There will be many people sent into your life to teach you many, many things; you must learn to recognize these people."*

Mom said with her smile, taking Christina's hand into hers.

*"Yea, yea, yea; mom, you already told me that, now tell me where I can find Sera."*

Christina said, squatting down beside her mom and giving her a serious look.

*"I don't know sweetheart, but you must not stop looking for her; some things we are not meant to know."*

Mom whispered, giving Christina a look that said "sorry"; as she stood.

*"Yea, yea, yea; we wouldn't want to screw up the big plan."*

Christina said, looking at her mom with sarcasm prominent in her voice as she stood up with her mom.

*"Don't you ever take that sort of tone with me young lady."*

Mom demanded, as she looked in-to Christina's eyes; disappointment prominent in her voice, as she took Christina into her embrace.

*"I'm sorry mom; I'm really sorry."*

Christina said, as she reached her arms around her mother.

"O.K. sweetheart, I have to go now; I love you."

Mom gently said, giving Christina a loving kiss on her lips.

"I love you mom."

Christina whispered, as her dream began to fade.

Christina woke up and lay still for a few moments. She listened to the early birds chirping in the morning silence. Rosie and Stormy were still sleeping after their late night smoke-out. Christina slowly exited her tent with a hard stretch. She looked around the camp and then she started the chore of rekindling the fire to cook breakfast.

"Good morning Christina."

Stormy said, exiting his tent and walking over toward Christina.

"*Good morning dumb-ass.*"

Christina casually said, continuing her chore of building the fire.

"*And you want me to teach you to track.*"

Stormy said point-blank, stopping and staring at Christina.

"*I'm sorry, I'm sorry, I will only call you Stormy from now on.*"

Christina quickly said, as she pulled Stormy into a hug.

"*Thank you, now come with me and I will show you a few tricks on tracking.*"

Stormy said, taking Christina by the hand and heading into the woods.

"*Wait, wait; my bow.*"

Christina said, as she went to retrieve her bow-and-arrows.

Christina began to learn the art of the trackers. Not so much as to track for food, but to learn how to erase her own tracks just in case she were ever to be tracked. Stormy understood what Christina was wanting to learn.

Rosie had woken and was sitting by the fire waiting for the tracking team to return from the hunt. She already had most of the camp packed and ready to go. The only things that were not packed were the things that they would need for cooking breakfast.

# BACK-WOODS
## BY- RAYDON COOLEY

LIVING IN THE BACK-WOODS
LAID UP IN THE SHADE
NO ONE COMES TO SEE ME
AND I LIKE IT THAT WAY
MY WOMAN SHE'S A LADY
STAYS HERE BY MY SIDE
PROMISED THAT SHE'D LOVE ME
UNTIL THE DAY WE DIE
THE CHILDREN THEY HAVE MARRIED
AND DONE MOVED INTO TOWN
I GUESS WE'LL GET TO SEE THEM
WHEN THE RIVERS GO DOWN
    BUT FOR NOW
I'M LIVING IN THE BACK-WOODS
LAID UP IN THE SHADE
NO ONE COMES TO SEE ME
AND I LIKE IT THAT WAY

# CHAPTER EIGHT
## CABIN IN THE MOUNTAINS

Christina and Rosie were riding side-by-side as Stormy brought up the rear. Rosie glanced back over her shoulder to make sure Stormy could not hear her speaking to Christina.

"We can't take him all the way to the cabin, you do know that right?"

Rosie quietly said, turning her eyes straight up ahead.

"What are you talking about; he is going to be your new son-in-law."

Christina said, turning and giving Rosie one of her strange sideways look.

"What "IN THE HELL" are you talking about?"

Rosie demanded, bringing SNOWFLAKE to a sudden and complete stop.

"Wait, I didn't tell you about my dream a few days ago did I?"

Christina giggled in a question form, quickly bringing BLACKWALL to a stop and looking back at Rosie.

"NO! I do not believe that you did."

Rosie quickly responded, giving one of her disappointing looks toward Christina.

"Well, if I'm a true dreamer, as you say I am, then he is going to be your new son-in-law."

Christina informed Rosie, with a big smile and a twinkle in her eye.

"Is everything alright ladies?"

Stormy asked, riding up beside the two girls and pulling his horse to a stop.

"Hell no, everything is not alright; now get your ass back, this is girl talk."

Rosie said angrily, giving Stormy a go to hell look, and pointing back down the trail.

"Yes ma'am; "sorry."

Stormy said sarcastically, turning and heading back down the trail.

"That is what my little girl wants?"

Rosie said in a question form, staring at his back as he slowly rode back down the trail.

*"Your little girl has her own little girl, and he is going to make her extremely happy."*

Christina proudly said, turning and leaning forward in the saddle and continuing up the trail.

Rosie quickly followed, occasionally glancing over to see Christina with a great big smile on her face. Rosie would turn and look over her shoulder and then turn her head back up the trial, shaking it side-to side. Christina would just giggle.

After several more days of fast hard riding through snow flurries and strong cold breezes, the daylight from the sun on this day was becoming dimmer than normal. Stormy quickly came riding up beside Rosie.

*"We need to set camp now."*

Stormy shouted above the wind, as he got as close as he could to Rosie.

*"I know damn-it; I know."*

Rosie shouted back, aggravated that she had to admit defeat to the weather so early in the day.

Rosie rode up beside Christina and pointed to a group of large trees just off the side of the trail. The trio quickly moved into the center of the trees and dismounted, than they began to unpack their tents.

"*NO!! No; we all must sleep in one tent.*"

Stormy demanded, yelling as loud as he could so to be heard over the howling winds.

"*Do you really think it's going to be that bad?*"

Rosie shouted, again not wanting to admit defeat.

"*Yes; and worse than that.*"

Stormy yelled, pulling a bit larger tent from his horse.

Rosie and Stormy began to securing the tent to the large sturdy trees that surrounded the camp. Christina held onto the three horses as she watched them battling with the tent against the strong wind. After Rosie and Stormy had won the battle, he pointed for Christina to get to the tent as he took the smaller tents from their places and began to wrap them around the horses, giving them some shelter from the freezing winds. Soon the trio was sitting in a small circle inside the tent wrapped in their sleeping bags. Rosie pulled out her pipe and gave Stormy a smile, Stormy followed suit.

"*Great, trapped with two druggies.*"

Christina giggled, as she pulled her sleeping-bag in around herself.

*"Sweetheart, I am going to get so stoned tonight, you will not know who or where you are."*

Rosie said with a loud giggle, as she pulled out one of her lighters.

*"I don't think so, I'm not smoking any."*

Christina said, rocking back and forth to create warmth in her sleeping-bag.

*"Babe, you don't have to smoke it, just breathe it."*

Rosie giggled, and then sparked up her pipe.

Christina's eyes became very large as Stormy sparked up his pipe and the tent began to fill with smoke. Soon Christina was completely out of it as Stormy and Rosie started chanting their favorite songs.

## [REALISTIC DREAM]

Tonight Christina dreams that she is out on a warm beach building big sandcastles with her mom. They can hear a radio playing Native American songs off in the distance.

*"There is a very bad snow storm coming tonight mom."*

Christina informs her mom, as she continues to sculpt the sand-castle.

*"Yes, I know sweetheart, but we will be fine here where it's warm and sunny."*

Mom explained, momentary look over at Christina with a warm smile as she helped with the sandcastle.

*"Mom, I miss you so much; and dad; and Sera."*

Christina said, stopping for just a moment and gently taking her mom by the hand.

*"Yes Dear, and we miss you just as much."*

Mom softly whispered, reaching over and pulling Christina into her caring embrace.

*"Where is dad? I want to see him."*

Christina said, giving her mom a curious look.

*"Well, he is busy with something important."*

Mom explained, returning to her building of the sandcastle.

*"More important than me."*

Christina said sarcastically, as she returned to the sandcastle.

*"I'm sure it has something to do with you."*

Mom said, and then began to hum along with the songs playing in the distance.

*"Like what?"*

Christina quickly insisted, excited that dad was doing something for her.

*"I have already said too much, now let's just enjoy the warm sunny day together."*

Mom said, and then she began to hum again.

*"Yea; Yea; Yea; THE BIG PLAN."*

Christina exclaimed with extreme sarcasm, holding her

hands as far apart as she could.

"*CHRISTINA!!!*"

Mom shouts, looking up with pain written all over her face.

"*I'm sorry; I'm sorry; I'm sorry.*"

Christina sincerely apologized, as she reached and took her mom into a tight embrace.

"*It's O.K. babe; now it's time for me to go.*"

Mom said, as she gave Christina a kiss.

"*Can you tell dad I love and miss him?*"

Christina asked, looking up into her mother's eyes.

*"Yes, I promise I will do that; I love you."*

Mom said.

**CHRISTINA'S DREAM BEGINS TO FADE.**

Christina woke up with her head in a slight spin, as she attempts to focus her eyes she can see a tiny dim glimpse of light on a small spot on the tent. Her mind begins to remember the toking party that she had no choice but to participate in last-night.

*"Are you guys still alive?"*

Christina asked quietly, and then she lay still listening for a minute.

*"Damn-it, I hope you two didn't O.D."*

Christina whispered, sitting up and staring at the tiny glow on the small spot on the tent.

*"You can't O.D. on marijuana."*

Rosie said with a giggle, as Stormy joined in with a chuckle.

Christina slowly moves to the lighted spot on the tent and found the door opening and pulled the flap back.

"What the hell is this!?"

Christina demanded in a question, looking down a six foot long tunnel just big enough for a person to crawl through.

"It's the way out."

Stormy said, sitting up and looking as the sun light came pouring down through the tunnel.

"How did that happen?"

Christina asked, with a curious sound in her voice.

"Rosie and I took turns last-night while you were enjoying your buzz."

Stormy said, with a bit of sarcasm in his voice.

"Yea, I did enjoy last-night."

Christina said, with a pleasant and happy go lucky voice, starting to crawl into the neat tunnel.

"Wait, you had a dream didn't you."

Rosie asked, reaching and grabbing a hold of Christina's leg.

"Yes, yes I did."

Christina giggled, as she kicked loose from Rosie's grip, and quickly went toward the light.

Rosie and Stormy were right behind Christina. The sun was shining bright as the three exited the tunnel. The horses were clear of snow and ice, as they stood wrapped like a three layer taco in their tent covering.

*"O.K. no breakfast this morning, get the sleeping-bags and let's get moving."*

Rosie said, heading for the horses to unwrap the taco looking tent.

*"Wait a damned minute, we have to dig out my tent."*

Stormy protested loudly, standing and staring at Rosie.

*"No, you don't need the tent anymore, we will be home before dark."*

Rosie explained, as she began the task of unwrapping the horses.

*"You will be home, but I will need this tent in the future."*

Stormy insisted, crossing his arms across his chest and refusing to move.

*"No, Stormy you won't, you will be staying with me and my daughter; Christina had a dream."*

Rosie informed Stormy, standing with her arms crossed and staring at Stormy.

"Christina had a dream."

Stormy said point-blank.

"Yes, a dream, now go get the damned sleeping-bags."

Rosie said, and then continued to prepare the horses.

"My dad warned me that women were crazy."

Stormy said, as he started through the tunnel to retrieve the sleeping-bags.

The rest of the day was spent at a fast pace, the warm sun was quickly melting the snow. As late afternoon was approaching Rosie began to get excited. The aroma of a fire-place started to fill the air. When they topped a ridge over-looking the small cabin, Rosie put SNOWFLAKE into a hard fast run. Christina pulled BLACKWALL to a halt, and signaled Stormy to stop. Rosie's daughter had heard the sound of the horse's hoofs pounding the ground and looked out the window to see her mother coming home. She quickly ran out the door and met Rosie in the front yard. Christina and Stormy sat upon the ridge and watched as the two held onto each-other.

"WOW. ~ That's her daughter?"

Stormy whispered in amassment, staring at a younger version of Rosie.

"*Yap.*"

Christina said, than she leaned forward in the saddle and put BLACKWALL into a slow walk.

Rosie and her daughter kept one arm around each-other as they turned and watched Christina and Stormy as they dismounted. Both Rosie and her daughter had wet faces from all of the tears that were still streaming from their eyes.

"*A brave; you have a brave.*"

Rosie's daughter said with excitement, turning and giving her mom a shocked look.

"*Yes dear, I found him wondering around in the woods and I thought of you.*"

Rosie said, giving Christina a wink and smile.

"*So I get to keep him mom? Really mom, I get to keep him.*"

Rosie's daughter said, holding tight onto her mother's arm, bouncing up and down like she had just gotten a new puppy.

"*He will need a lot of training sweetheart.*"

Rosie said with a slight giggle.

*"I will train him mom, I promise, I will train him."*

Rosie's daughter said, looking deep into her mother's eyes still holding onto her arm.

*"O.K. come here Stormy, I want you to meet Misty."*

Rosie said, holding her hand out and signaling for Stormy to come.

Christina broke into a hard laugh, as Stormy slowly moved toward the two women.

*"What the hell is so funny?"*

Rosie asked, Looking over at Christina and giving her a big smile.

*"Rosie, Stormy, misty; I can't wait to hear your granddaughter's name."*

Christina said, as she kept giggling.

*"Her name is Violet."*

Misty said, taking a hold of her new brave and spinning him around, giving him a once over.

*"What did you expect, Jane, or Paula; we are Indian."*

Rosie explained, giving Christina the signal to come closer.

*"Wait; how in the hell did she know that I have a daughter?"*

Misty asked, giving Christina a strange look.

"This is Christina; she is a true dreamer Misty."

Rosie said, as she introduced the two.

"Yes; Yes, I saw you; not too long ago. Standing on the porch and watching me and Violet play."

Misty said, slightly tilting her head and staring at Christina.

"Yes, she has that gift to, but she refuses to try and use it."

Rosie explained, gently taking Christina by the hand.

"Trust me Christina I understand, I refuse to use mine also."

Misty said, and then she gave her mom a tight hug and then started toward the cabin with a tight grip on her new brave.

"Thank you for my new brave mom, now you put the horses into the barn and I'm going to go and give my brave a bath."

Misty excitingly said, looking back over her shoulder as she pulled her new brave toward the house.

"Well, I guess we better take our time."

Rosie whispered, slowly starting toward the barn with Christina right behind.

Christina followed Rosie to the barn and began to remove BLACKWALL'S saddle.

"Rosie, Is Misty going to have sex with Stormy? I mean they just met."

Christina asked in a quiet voice, as if Misty might hear her.

"You are a virgin aren't you?"

Rosie asked with a slight giggle, as she walked SNOWFLAKE into her stall.

"UA; Yea!"

Christina exclaimed, as if that was the most stupid question that she had ever been asked.

"Well sweetheart, the day will come when you will meet that special man, and then it will be more addictive than any drug. And if you lose him you will crave it even more."

Rosie explained to Christina, as they put hay into the stalls.

"I'm going to wait a long, long time before I do that."

Christina informed Rosie, following her out of the barn.

"That would be a smart thing to do babe."

Rosie said, as they wrapped an arm around each-other as they slowly walked toward the house.

## *Growing up*

Christina's twentieth birthday came and went as she spent the winter with Rosie and her family in up-state New York. Joyful that she had another group of people she could call family. Stormy and Misty shared a love as deep as Christina had ever seen between two people. When spring sprung Misty informed everyone that Violet was going to be have a sibling. Christina hoped that she would see them again.

Now that spring had sprung and Christina said her good-by's, once again she continued on her quest to find her sister Sera. Over the next ten years she developed into an expert at tracking and hunting; and at eluding the U.N. DEMON'S and radical gangs. She consistently made the full circle from Pennsylvania down to Texas and then up to Washington. Making sure to stop and visit each one of her new families each time. Every time she would start to get discouraged in her quest, her mom always came to her in dreams and reminded her about "THE BIG PLAN." "You must keep searching for Sera" her mother would say. Christina was beginning to argue with her mother about the situation. After fourteen years of none stop searching for Sera, she was growing tired of the chase. Christina wanted desperately to stop and find a good man, and have her own family and daughter that she could love.

# BY THE BLOOD OF JESUS

## BY- RAYDON COOLEY

I WAS BORN
BY THE BLOOD OF JESUS
I PRAISE THE LORD
FOR SAVING MY SOLE
CRU-CI-FIED
FOR ALL US SINNERS
BUT ON THE THIRD DAY
I KNOW THAT HE ROSE
HE WALKS WITH ME
THROUGH THE VALLEY
HE SHINES HIS LIGHT
EVERYWHERE I GO
HE PROMISED ME
A PLACE IN HEAVEN
A PAR-A-DISE
WHERE I CAN REST MY SOLE
I WAS BORN
BY THE BLOOD OF JESUS
I PRAISE THE LORD
FOR SAVING MY SOLE
CRU-CI-FIED
FOR ALL US SINNERS
BUT ON THE THIRD DAY
I KNOW THAT HE ROSE

# CHAPTER NINE
## BIG RED DOG.

Christina has been on her quest to find Sera for the last fourteen years. This year, 2095, on her final journey between south Texas, and Seattle Washington, Christina will re-discover her faith in religion and the family that she has always dreamed of, and the man that she will marry.

She will discover that Sometimes, God will go above and beyond your prayers, and She will also complete her part of THE BIG PLAN.

Christina is now thirty years old and a beauty, five feet eleven in. tall, wavy blond hair and deep blue eyes. One hundred and forty five lb.'s of pure muscle. To survive now days, with no law to help guide society, staying in great shape is a must.

Christina slowly walks BLACKWALL across the bridge that leads out onto Surfside Texas. She knows there will be no-one at the beach house waiting. It's been five years since she has been here, the tide and storms have cleaned the beach of all the burnt down houses that once scattered the beach. There was still a bit of a chill in the breeze coming off the gulf waters this early in March. Christina dismounts and ties BLACKWALL to the rusty rail on the sagging deck, and then she slowly begins the chore of unpacking and giving BLACKWALL his rub down as she whistles his favorite tune, his hair now has speckles of gray, but Christina was thankful he was still healthy and in perfect shape. She picks up the door that has rotted off its hinges and tosses it onto the beach, and then carries her supplies into the house.

*"This is a big bag of shit."*

Christina whispered, sitting up her screen tent in the living-room with tear filled eyes, than she climbed into it and faded off to sleep for the night.

For the next several days Christina would sit on the beach and fish, and cry; and fish, and cry. She had started to become a little depressed and felt that life had not been fair to her. Every night she would cry herself to sleep.

A big shiny ball of orange slowly begins to rise up over the horizon. The air is crisp, coming across the bay early this morning. A light breeze crosses the sand. Christina is standing out on the deck of her family's

Texas beach house, watching endless waves softly kissing the dry Sand as the sun glistens across the gulf. After fourteen years of relentless searching, Christina has come to the conclusion that she probably will never locate her sister Sera. Christina also knows that there is nothing else worthwhile, except to continue her quest. She has been here at the beach-house for six days now. Staying in one place too long is a dangerous thing to do. She decides that it is time for her to head toward Washington.

*"Sera's not here this time either."*

Christina whispered, staring out across the gulf at the sun glistening off the water.

*"I'll leave tomorrow."*

Christina whispers, letting her mind reminisce about all the time when she and Sera would build sandcastles in the sand out on the beach, back when they were seven and eight years old.

*"I miss you so much Sera."*

Christina whispers, as the tears begin sliding down her cheeks.

Christina begins to feel the heat from the hot sun upon her bare skin. She turned, and walked through the hole where the door had once stood. She slowly walked through the living room, realizing exactly how bad the beach house has decayed over the last fourteen years.

*"I won't be coming back here."*

Christina said softly, looking around at all the broken windows and sagging floors.

Christina wondered down the short hallway, she stops at the doorway that leads into the room where her father spent a lot of his time.

*"Dad's study."*

Christina said softly, than she wondered into the room with the morning sun shining through the only window that was still in one piece.

She smiles at the CD player lying in the desk drawer, knowing it was beyond working. She gazed over the bookshelf behind her dad's solid oak desk that covered the back wall from top to bottom and corner to corner, Christina freezes into place as she spy's a particular book.

*"Dad's favorite book."*

Christina whispered, standing up on her tippy toes to retrieve the book from its place on the top shelf.

Her eyes fill with water as she gently rubs her finger across the raised white letters that's on the black covering. "Holy bible" is what she reads. Christina hears a thud sound where the book had been. She carefully moved the footstool into place and then she steps up to take a look.

"*A bottle.*"

Christina thought to herself, and then she reached in and pulled the bottle from its little cubby-hole.

"*BLACK VELVET.*"

Christina said, as she read the label on the bottle out loud.

"*But, dad didn't drink.*"

Christina whispered; then she gazed toward her dad's empty chair behind his desk.

"*DAD!*"

Christina said loudly, than she embraced the book and the bottle, as she stared up at the ceiling with tears drifting down her cheeks.

Christina returns into the living room and pulls her cut-off blue jean shorts and a bikini top from the saddle-bag, than she considers that there is not anyone around for many a mile. She decides to spend this one last day wearing only her birthday-suit. Christina remembers the beach umbrella that is tucked safely away in the hall closet. She quickly retrieves the umbrella then went out onto the deck and opened it up and took a seat on her beach towel, with both the book, and the bottle in her hand. She opened both of them, and then listened to the continuous waves softly kissing the sand, she spent the rest of the day reading, drinking and sunning.

*"Thou shall not kill."*

Christina whispered, as she examines a passage in the book.

*"Well God, Times have changed."*

Christina said loudly, turning the bottle up to her lips as she sat considering the passage that she had just read.

As the sun disappeared below the horizon and darkness with its swarms of mosquitoes began to silently consume the beach, Christina was unable to stand and walk. After drinking a half a bottle of Black Velvet, she slowly crawled into her screen tent that she had set up in the living-room and went limp. The large amount of alcohol she had drank helped Christina sleep better than she had in a long, long time.

## [FAVORITE DREAM]

Christina's favorite dream comes again as she slips into a deep sleep tonight. It's the one with the small child, her pretty daughter that she never had. The girl looked to be around seven or eight years old, with long straight coal black hair and big sparkling brown eyes. She seemed always to be happy as she played out in the front yard. Christina sits in a porch swing on a wrap-around porch of a big farm house, and watches as the tiny girl plays.

Sometimes Christina wondered about the small girl's appearance, Christina has long blond hair and blue eyes, but she still cherished the dream.

This morning wasn't very crisp; in fact it was starting out to be a warm morning. Christina lay in her screen tent, trying to focus her Black Velvet blood shot eyes.

"There is something red in the corner."

Christina thought out loud, making her best attempt at forcing her eyes to focus.

"S H I T!"

Christina whispers quietly, feeling that cold chill, running down her spin.

When Christina's eyes began to focus, she saw a large clump of red hair with a black nose and two large brown eyes staring back at her from across the room.

"Do not move."

Christina told herself, as she lay still, as still as she possibly could.

It was a big red dog, a very big red dog. It weighed at least one hundred lb. with the looks of a survivor.

"I need a weapon."

Christina thought; franticly looking around with only her eyes moving.

*"Nothing."*

Christina whispers, and then she turned her eyes back toward the dog.

The big red dog cautiously stands and then stretches, reaching out with his front paws as far as they would go, and then shook back into his stance, never taking his eyes off Christina. This giant of a dog had bulging muscles that seem to roll across his firm body as he slowly walked across the room. He slowly began moving toward Christina with his big eyes still locked onto her position. As he approached the screen tent, he lies down and then slipped his nose under the edge of the screen and just laid there.

*"Please, don't bite me."*

Christina said, staying transfixed, staring at the little wet shinny black nose.

Big Red began to sweep the floor with the long red hair attached to his huge tail, looking up at Christina with two large sad brown eyes, as his black noise sniffed the air. Christina slowly sat up, and crossed her legs Indian style. She looked into his big brown eyes as he lay still with just his tail swinging back and forth, then she began to move her hand in slow motion. Very slowly she began to move her hand toward the large red dog. When she reached his little black shinny nose she started to gently rub it with her fingers. The dog began to lick her hand with a small whine. After a few minutes, Christina set back up.

"*Big Red.*"

Christina said softly, as if she was giving the big red dog a name.

"*Can I get up now?*"

Christina asks, slowly rising up, still keeping her eyes locked on Big Red.

Big Red quickly jumps to his feet and gives a very loud bark, then turns and prances out onto the deck with his beautiful long red hair flowing across his muscled body, and clicking his toe-nails across the hard wood floor as if he was doing it on purpose as he went.

"*BLACKWALL!*"

Christina gasps, ducking out from under her screen tent, concerned about her horse.

Christina runs over to the living room table, and retrieved a hunting knife from the inside of her saddle bag, than she cautiously walks toward the deck. Christina slowly peeks around the edge of the door frame where the door once stood. BLACKWALL was still tied to the corner of the deck.

Christina steps out onto the deck. Big Red was lying beside half a bottle of Black Velvet and her father's favorite book. Christina curiously stared towards Big Red for a moment.

*"I'm going to go get dressed."*

Christina said, realizing that she was standing with a knife in her hand, in the buff.

Big Red stared out across the bay not even paying any attention to Christina as she turned and went back into the house to get dressed.

Christina slowly packed up camp onto the back of BLACKWALL this morning with difficulty. She was experiencing a variety of emotions. Christina knew that she would never be coming back here again. She empty's out one of her waterproof saddle bags, and then puts her Fathers favorite book into the bag along with the half-bottle of Black Velvet. Christina carefully attaches the bag onto the saddle on the back of BLACKWALL.

*"Brazes river, water, Fishing, and Hunting, a girl has to eat."*

Christina thought out loud, turning and then heading BLACKWALL northwest, toward Seattle Washington.

Christina noticed that Big Red had decided that he would join her and BLACKWALL, on their very last trip they would be taking between Texas, and Washington. Big Red constantly ran way out in the front, as if he were assuring a safe passage. Stopping and looking back from time to time with his ears and tail straight up, he would wait for Christina to catch up. Then up the trail he would run again.

*"This dog has been well trained."*

Christina said, noticing how keen he was of his surroundings.

Big Red would always scout around the area when Christina began to set camp. He would take wide circles around, sniffing every strange smell. Christina would set up her screen tent and build a fire-pit and then gathered firewood; she would smile as she watched Big Red mark his territory for the night. Christina and Big Red grew secure with one another over the next several weeks. Big Red always slept halfway in-between Christina and BLACKWALL as if he had been sent to be their protector. Christina seemed to be sleeping better now knowing Big Red was there.

    Today begins as a sunny and warm day. The slight breeze that was blowing helped to dry the sweat. Christina slowly rode along enjoying the day. She had begun to softly whistle a soothing tune that BLACKWALL especially liked, causing his ears to stand and to put a bit more style in his step. Christina realizes she has not seen Big Red for a while. She stands way up high in the stirrup and looks up the trail. She gives a loud whistle, but there is no Big Red. Christina whistles once again, but still no Big Red to be seen.

*"This doesn't feel right."*

    Christina said, than she dismounts and gives a loud whistle.

    A big red ball of hair came over the hill at a hard run, coming to a stop in front of Christina. Big Red was completely out of breath, like he had been running for a long distance; he looks up at Christina as he caches his breath.

*"Where you been?"*

    Christina scolded, staring down at Big Red with a hard look.

Big Red gives a large puff of air from deep down inside, then he stares up at Christina with his tail and his ears straight up, then he turned his attention up the trail.

"What, is there trouble?"

Christina asked, reaching and retrieving her binoculars from the saddle, and then she climbed up a tall tree to get a good look up the trail.

"U. N. DEMON"S!"

Christina said loudly, down to Big Red as if he knows how to speak English.

When Christina was in her teens, these men were once everywhere. The U.S. Government brought them into the country when the local law had quit, and all religion had been outlawed by the U.N. Most of these men could not speak English. "U.N. DEMON'S" is what her father had called them, the worst of the worse. Christina had learned to avoid these men at all cost.

"These men have never read thou shall not kill."

Christina whispered, quickly climbing down the tree.

"We got to go my friend's."

Christina said with a tremble in her voice, as she mounted BLACKWALL, then she hurried back down the trail.

Big Red took the lead as Christina followed with BLACKWALL. After a short time Big Red took a right turn into thick, tall bushes.

"Where in the hell are you going?"

Christina growled at Big Red, watching the thick bushes swallow him up.

Big Red gives a loud deep bark, as if to say follow me.

"And I was thinking that you were a smart dog."

Christina bolstered, standing high up in the stirrups, trying to get a look at Big Red through the thick bushes.

Big Red gave another loud deep bark then kept going.

"O.K.-O.K.- I'm coming."

Christina said, turning BLACKWALL and then crashed through the thick bushes behind Big Red.

"Mosquitoes, Spiders, and Snakes, I do not like this situation Big Red."

Christina proclaims, pulling her feet up onto the back of BLACKWALL.

For the next two hours Christina, Big Red, and BLACKWALL push their way through the thick brush and low limbs, Christina was thankful when the landscape had cleared. Big Red had led them to a small river. Christina decided to stop beside the small river for the night.

*"Setting up camp right here."*

Christina said, as she dismounts then began to unsaddle BLACKWALL.

Big Red follows Christina to the river as she leads BLACKWALL.

{ Bath time.}

*"Big Red, you are a smart dog."*

Christina told Big Red, as they bathed, and played in the cool water.

Camp was set with fish for dinner, enough daylight left to read dads book a little. Christina pulls the book from its leather bag, and her dad's half a bottle of Black Velvet. Christina sat with her back leaning against the saddle, and opened the bottle and the book. Big Red came and sat in front of Christina, staring up at her with his sad eyes, as he gave a small whiny bark.

*"What!"*

Christina asks, looking over at Big Red, and then she took a drink from the bottle.

Big Red gave another whining bark and he continued staring at Christina.

*"What, you want me to read to you, out loud?"*

Christina asked, staring at Big Red with a surprised look on her face.

Big Red slowly lay his head down on top of Christina's feet with his ears straight up.

*"I can't believe I'm doing this."*

Christina proclaimed, and then she continued to read, out loud as per request.

After she had been reading a few minutes she looked up and took a drink, then held the bottle in the direction of Big Red.

*"You want some of this to?"*

Christina asked with sarcasm in her voice, as she looks over at Big Red.

Big Red gave a loud sneeze, and then shook his head and looked away.

*"O.K. Smartass."*

Christina said, and then returned to reading out loud to Big Red.

Big Red laid his head back down on her feet and listened to Christina read until the sun had gone down.

Christina lay in her screen tent staring up at the stars. She began to meditate upon what she had read. She was trying to understand what it was that made her father loved this book so.

*"That makes no since, how can the woman get herself pregnant without having sex?"*

Christina pondered, as her eyes began to get heavy with sleep.

*"Can't happen!"*

Christina proclaims, and then she begins to drift off into a deep sleep.

## [FAVORITE DREAM RETURNS]

Christina sat out on the front porch and watches her beautiful daughter with long black hair, and big brown eyes.

*"Mom, come play with me."*

Her daughter insisted, as she chased a big green beach ball across the yard.

*"O. K. Sweetheart."*

Christina said, as she rose up from the porch swing and begins to play ball with her beautiful little girl.

As Christina wakes, the sun is rising above the horizon. She lay still relishing the memory of the dream for a few moments.

The morning brought another hot day. The sun was bright rising above the horizon. Christina begins to break camp as Big Red disappeared into the woods, going to look for breakfast Christina figured. Christina always took care when rolling up her screen tent, the only protection that she had against mosquitoes and all of the night crawling bugs. Camp was packed and put upon the back of BLACKWALL, when Big Red came running up to Christina and gave one of his deep down puffs of air, then he turned and looked north with his ears and his tail standing straight up. Christina immediately climbed up a tree with her binoculars in hand. Christina's heart stopped when she seen the smoke rising above the trees, she focused her binoculars.

*"One... two..three...four... five."*

Christina whispered, counting the five U.N. DEMON'S out loud.

*"Damn it all to hell."*

Christina demands, quickly climbing down the tree trembling with fear.

Christina puts her foot into the stirrup, than up onto the back of BLACKWALL she went. She looked down at Big Red.

*"Go west young man.... Go west."*

Christina said, turning BLACKWALL and then leaning forward into the saddle.

BLACKWALL lunged into a hard run, as Big Red was keeping pace with the escape. Christina kept him at a hard run until she could feel his heavy breathing, then she slowed him to a fast walk. By midday the sky had became cloudy, and a slight mist of rain was beginning to fall. A light breeze from the north-west had the temperature cooled.

*"We need to allocate as much distance between us and them as possible."*

Christina said, keeping BLACKWALL at his constant fast pace.

After several days of extreme riding, Christina was confident that the DEMON'S were not in pursuit. Most of these men were heading south in order to escape the cold weather that would soon entrap the north. They would not be inclined to track anyone headed north.

*"We have reached the plains of north Texas."*

Christina informed Big Red, Noticing fewer trees and more open space.

Windmills have started to appear all across the landscapes. Back when the electromagnetic pulse zapped out all electricity, People built these so to pump water, most were still working. They were built extremely tough. As the day came to a close Christina came across one that was still working.

*"Setting up camp."*

Christina gladly announced, as she dismounts BLACKWALL, and then she began to unsaddle and rubbed him down, whistling a soothing tune.

    The night air is now perfect for sleeping, it's not too hot and it's not too cold. Christina was thankful the sky had cleared. She could count the stars as she lay in her screen tent drifting off to sleep.

**{Christina's dream is not pleasant}**

She was in a flat desert plain and there was no place she could find to hide, too many U. N. DEMON'S were in fast pursuit, and no matter which way she tried turning, there was additional DEMON'S coming straight toward her. Christina was riding around in circles, as she tried staying out ahead of them. Christina was overflowing with terror, BLACKWALL was breathing way too hard. If she did not stop soon he would not last much longer, but the DEMON'S were beginning to close in on her and Christina had begun crying hard. Tears streamed down her face as BLACKWALL was tiring and beginning to slow down.

*"It was only a dream......It was only a dream."*

Christina kept telling herself, as she gained control of her trembling and shallow breathing.

Although Christina slept on top of her sleeping bag in the buff and the morning air was cool, she was still soaked with sweat. After she had gained control of her nerves, Christina went over to the windmill and stood up under the water spout, taking herself a relaxing shower, washing away her anxiety. The sun began peeking up above the edge of the horizon as Christina finished getting dressed. Christina packed camp upon to the back of BLACKWALL. She climbs the windmill with her binoculars in hand. Christina knew that the DEMON'S were on their southern migration, so she would find a high spot and scout up ahead several times a day. Christina could see forever in this flat part of the country, and she could not see anything to be concerned about. Christina decides to have an easy day, taking the time to hunt small varmints that came her way. Every couple of hours she would take the time to stop and rinse herself off underneath a windmill. The last time Christina had made this trip she had gone west through the desert, she wasn't going to make that mistake again. This time she had decided that she would go northwest up toward Reno Nevada.

    Christina arrived at the nest working windmill as dusk crept across the landscape. Christina set camp, than cooked two rabbits she had managed to spear earlier in the day, than a deserving long shower underneath the water spout. Tonight was another perfect night, not to hot and not to cold. Big Red and Christina sat by the fire for a time, Christina would talk to Big Red as if he were a person, and Big Red would give a whiny moan as if he was carrying on the conversation. When the flames had became a bed of red coals, Christina climbed into her screen tent and faded off into a deep sleep as Big Red took his sleeping place between Christina and BLACKWALL.

## [TWILIGHT]

The morning sun was just minutes below the horizon. Christina was awakened by the constant barking. Big Red was standing on the south side of the tower barking towards the way that they had came the day before.

*"This better be damned important."*

Christina demanded, aggravated by the loud early disturbance of a peaceful sleep.

Christina sat up and looked to see what was up. She could see the mosquitoes flying around the tent were the size of horse flies. She climbed out from her tent, retrieving her binoculars from the saddle, she climbed up the windmill.

*"One,-two,-three-,four,-five six,.* **Six U.N. DEMON'S."**

Christina whispers, watching in terror as the six DEMON'S were heading straight for her.

*"SHIT...SHIT...SHIT."*

Christina kept saying, quickly climbing down as fast as she could.

*"10 miles... 10 miles... 10 miles."*

Christina kept saying, as she packed up fast, as fast as possible; wading up her screen tent into a ball and stuffing it into the saddle bag.

*"No time, got to move. No time, got to move."*

Christina kept repeating, with fear present in her voice, as she mounts upon BLACKWALL. Christina leans forward as BLACKWALL lunged into a fast run.

*"G O... G O... G O."*

Christina repeated, as the terrifying survival mode kicked in.

*"Big Red! ~~ No Big Red!"*

Christina shouted to no avail, looking back to see Big Red at a hard run south, toward the direction of the DEMON'S.

BLACKWALL could out run the wind and he was giving it everything he had. Christina was sure she could stay ahead of the DEMON'S, even gain some ground. But she also knew that they would never give up until they lost her trail. They have nothing better to do but to enjoy the chase.

*"We will have to lose them."*

Christina told BLACKWALL, looking back toward the horizon; desperately searching for a red spot.

U. N. DEMON'S are not very experienced at tracking, unless there was an elder tracker, ones that were in the war. There's not too many left, but they were good. Christina learned this the hard way. It had taken her a month to lose an elder a couple years ago, but that was up in Tennessee then down through Louisiana. This is flat land with no place you can hide.

*"If we go west, there are canyons in New Mexico. It's a three week ride. We will lose them there."*

Christina explained, than she turned BLACKWALL and headed west.

The next three weeks Christina pushed hard, a fast trot for five minutes, walk for five minutes. Then she would stop at a windmill, for a fifteen minute water break and rest, every three hours or so. For the next three weeks this was Christina's and BLACKWALL'S routine from sunup until sunset. Every night when she set up camp tears would begin to stream down her face as her mind wonder about the fate of Big Red. Christina knew that he had gone back in order to slow down the DEMON'S to give her a head start on her escape.

*"Let's turn north, and lose those bastards."*

Christina suggested to BLACKWALL with a smile, knowing she had won this round. Christina set for a few minutes scouting for a red spot, but there was no Big Red.

Every evening when she began to set up camp, she would constantly look around and imagine Big Red sniffing every tree and every bush within his circle around the camp, and the way he always marked his territory. She began to tremble as she felt the empty spot deep down in her gut. Every time she tried to read from dad's favorite book her eyes would begin to water, causing the words to blur together, as her mind's eye gave a picture of Big Red laying with his head on her feet with his ears perked up, listening as she would read out loud.

Every morning Christina would search the horizon for a red spot, and then she would turn BLACKWALL and headed north looking through her watery eyes. Several streams were now filled with the rain water from all the fall rains and maneuvering through them was now becoming extremely dangerous. But not nearly as dangerous as what was behind them.

Fall was definitely in the air this morning as the sun peaked up above the horizon. Christina could feel the chill in the air as she packed up camp. She climbed a tall tree with her binoculars and looked back to the south, still no Big Red. Christina noticed that dark clouds were forming to the northwest.

*"Bad storm comings, we need to find shelter my friend."*

Christina explained, as she put her foot into the stirrup and mounted BLACKWALL.

# CHAPTER TEN
## FARM HOUSE

Christina road hard the rest of the day, the canyons had now became large rolling valleys. She sat up on top of a ridge overlooking the huge valley. Christina enjoys the serene mountainous scenery, than she scouted through her binoculars and examined a farm house across the valley.

*"S H I T...S H I T...S H I T."*

Christina mumbled, watching as this old man fed his chickens out behind the barn.

*"What in the hell, it looks like he is feeding the chicken's."*

Christina proclaimed, taking a moment to give BLACKWALL a strange sideways look.

Christina, continued to watch the old man, she begins to hear loud thunder rumbling across the darkening sky.

*"U. N. DEMON'S don't tend to animals. We need shelter; Now!"*

Christina suggest, as she mounts BLACKWALL and begins toward the farm house with the old man feeding chickens.

Christina began to consider the situation as she advanced toward the house. She knows that the U.N. DEMON'S do not stay in one place, and they definitely did not tend to chickens. They just destroy everything and then move on. As she approached the farm house, the old man had moved to the front porch.

"OH...M Y....GOD...He has a gun."

Christina said quietly, keeping a close watch on the old man.

Christina had not seen a gun in many a year, most ammunition has become imposable to find, which had made gun obsolete. Christina saw the lighting strike the ground on top of the mountain. A strong wind began to blow as Christina brought BLACKWALL to a halt.

"That's close enough, I have bullets."

The old man said, aiming his gun straight at Christina.

"I'm not looking for trouble sir, just a place that I can take shelter from the storm, and then I'll be gone tomorrow morning."

Christina said, with her most sexy voice and the prettiest smile that she could muster, with her hands up in surrender.

"A wild U.N. beast!"

The man shouted, raising his gun up to his shoulder, looking past Christina.

Christina quickly turns to see a big red ball of hair in the distance, limping toward them from the direction she had just come.

*"NO! ~ NO!- BIG RED – BIG RED!"*

Christina shouted, than she turned, putting BLACKWALL and herself between the man and Big Red, than bolted toward Big Red.

Big Red immediately collapsed when he seen Christina coming fast to his rescue. Christina dismounts BLACKWALL before he came to a complete stop. Christina quickly set down on the ground and pulled Big Red into her lap, she had tears of happiness streaming down her face as she held Big Red in a tight embrace, burying her face deep into his hair. He had a few fresh scars where a sharp knife had made contact with his skin, no deep cuts just superficial battle scars. He was just completely exhausted from tracking Christina as fast as he could. Christina gently picked him up and placed him across the saddle as she mounted BLACKWALL behind Big Red, than she turned and started back toward the man that was waiting on the porch. Christina saw the lightning strike a tall tree way across the big valley as she brought BLACKWALL to a stop in front of the man on the porch. She turned her head when the wind begins to gust through the valley blowing dust into her face.

*"The dog sleeps in the barn."*

The old man demands, pointing toward the barn with a look of disbelief on his face.

*"That will be fine. I will sleep there as well."*

Christina said, turning her head from the strong wind once again.

Christina turned toward the barn, than her ears catches the sound of a woman's voice.

*"You come back to the house and eat dinner."*

The woman said, as she opened the door and stepped out onto the porch.

Christina turned back to the porch to see a sturdy woman, into her late sixty's stepping out onto the porch wiping her hands on her apron.

*"I don't want to be any trouble."*

Christina stated, not wanting to impose on the elderly couple.

*"I won't hear of it, now you go put the animals up then bring your butt back to the house."*

The woman demands, then she waved the back of her hand toward Christina.

*"Yes ma'am."*

Christina replied, and then she turns and starts in the direction of the barn.

Christina was impressed with the excellent condition that the barn was in as she opened the door and led BLACKWALL into the barn. She looked around as she laid Big Red down on a clump of hay. She noticed a good roof with sturdy walls, and plenty of feed and hay. The stall that she put BLACKWALL into was in excellent shape. Big Red was sound asleep before Christina had unsaddled and given BLACKWALL his hay.

*"This is a genuine farmer, and somehow he has managed to survive. I would be willing to bet his guns have something to do with that."*

Christina thought aloud, as she enjoyed the beauty of the other horses in the barn.

The storm had arrived with bright blinding flashes of lighting and loud clashes of thunder. A hard rain had begun to fall as

Christina steps upon the front porch and knocks on the door.

*"Hurry up, get in here before you catch your death of cold."*

The woman quickly said, opening the door and pulling Christina inside, handing her a warm dry towel.

*"Thank you, my name is Christina."*

Christina said, with bloodshot eyes from all her happy crying for Big Red, as she wiped the water from her hair.

*"My name is Mary, and grouch is Joe."*

Mary said, taking her by the hand and leading Christina toward the kitchen table.

It has been a long, long time since Christina attended a home-made dinner, with a real table, inside a real house with decent people, and she was very hungry. Christina's eyes began burning as she tries to hold back her tears as the elderly couple acquired one of her hands each, and then the man gave the blessing. She'd been a teenager the last time that she seen or heard anyone pray. Her memory begins to fill with the images of her father. Christina ate in silence, letting her mind take a stroll down memory lane. After dinner Joe went and sat on the porch, as Mary and Christina clean the kitchen.

*"Can I ask you about your dog?"*

Mary asked, as she washed the dishes and then handed them to Christina to rinse.

*"Yes, I was wondering what Joe meant by, U.N. beast."*

Christina said, continuing to rinse and dry the dishes as Mary handed them to her.

*"Those dogs were imported by the U.N. about ten years ago, they are highly intelligent and very fast and practically impossible to kill. Most were killed for food by their masters, and the rest have become wild, if this dog has accepted you as his master than you are a very lucky woman."*

Mary said, looking over at Christina with a big smile on her face.

*"I woke up one morning quite a while back, and he was just there; and he has saved my butt many times since, and I am not his master, I am his friend. I thought I lost him about a month ago. I am ~~ overwhelmed, to have him back.*

Christina said, as they finished up with the drying of the dishes.

*"Well, whatever you wish to call him, you are still a lucky woman to have that dog."*

Mary said, as she turned and looked at Joe standing at the door listening.

Christina gave her thanks, than she headed out through the door into the pouring rain, with this huge bright yellow rain coat which Joe insisted that she put over her head. Inside the barn it was calm and dry.

## {TIME TO SLEEP}

Tonight, Christina's dream is a nightmare. It starts out with Christina sitting on BLACKWALL outside of a small town. She watches in horror as the group of U. N. DEMON'S, terrorize the town. They burn and destroy everything in sight and killing everyone the U. N. DEMON'S can find. One of them spots Christina and started to give chase. She turned and runs as fast as she can get BLACKWALL to run. The DEMON begins to catch up. He begins to shout, but all Christina can hear coming from his mouth is a rooster crowing.

Christina wakes up to a rooster crowing out on the side of the barn.
"I hate those damned DEMON'S."
Christina said, sitting up and buried her face into her hands.
After she gets her breathing under control, Christina takes a peek outside the barn door. She sees Mary waiting on the front porch sitting in her favorite rocking chair.
"I guess we are not getting away that easy."
Christina said, as she puts the bright yellow rain coat over her shoulder and she and Big Red starts toward the house.
"Well, good morning pretty lady and a very good morning to you big red dog."

Mary said, giving her a big smile, amazed at the love that this dog has for Christina and how prevalent it was in his actions, staying close to Christina's side.

*"Good morning Mary, I brought back the coat and thank you for everything. I'll be on my way now."*

Christina said, laying the bright yellow coat on one of the rocking chairs.

*"Nnnooo...no. no. no.. You can't be going anywhere, you know today is the Sabbath."*

Mary said, holding up her bible and a cup of coffee.

Once again, Mary managed to trigger Christina's memory of her dad. She hasn't heard that word for what seems like an eternity.

*"But it's a perfect day for riding."*

Christina said, holding her hands palms up and looked to the sky.

*"No mater, today is for praying, singing, and talking to God, now would you like a hot cup of coffee?*

Mary proclaims, as she stood and went to the door, and then turned and waited for Christina to answer about the coffee.

*"Yes, I would love some coffee. I guess Big Red could use a little rest."*

Christina said, as she sat down in one of the rocking chairs, rubbing Big Red as he lay down next to her.

Mary went into the house and brought two cups of coffee back out.

*"Do you have a Bible?"*

Mary asks, holding out a hot cup of coffee for Christina.

*"Yes ma'am, it was my dads, but I find it just a little confusing."*

Christina said, taking the cup of coffee from Mary.

*"Well, you have to read it over and over then you will begin to understand."*

Mary told Christina, as if it were the truth; taking her seat and reached for her Bible.

*"Maybe that is why dad read it so much, so tell me how a woman who has never had sex, can still have a baby."*

Christina blurted out, before she could stop herself.

Christina turns, startled at the words that she heard coming from behind her. She had heard her dad saying those exact same words so, so many times when she was a teenager.

*"Anything is possible with the power of God."*

Joe said in a quiet soft voice, stepping out of the front door.

*"So can this power help me find my sister Sera?"*

Christina asks with hope in her voice, as she turned and looked up at Joe.

*"If you ask the right question, he will give you what you need."*

Joe said in a convincing voice, than he took a seat in his favorite rocking chair, and began to rock, giving Christina a convincing smile.

*"We will pray with you."*

Mary said, then reached and took a hold of Christina by the hand.

*"Tell me about your sister."*

Joe said, gently taking a hold of Christina's other hand.

*"She was my best friend, my hold world. When she turned eighteen, I was fourteen. That's when the U.S. police took her away and sent her to Seattle Washington to help and control the unrest in the area."*

Christina said, as Big Red began to lick her hand as if he could feel her emotions.

"Did you ever hear from her?"

Mary asked with watery eyes; finding it hard to hold back the tears.

"Yes, four times, and then the electricity went out and the U.N.DEMON'S began to round up all the Christians and my parents and I had to run."

Christina said, as she squeezed Mary's hand, the one that Big Red was still licking.

"So your family is Christian?"

Joe asks, releasing Christina's hand and then picking up his bible.

"Yes, my dad was a preacher, but my parents were killed when I was sixteen, and I have been searching for Sera ever since."

Christina said, as tears began to slowly slide down her cheeks.

"Let's sing some happy songs."

Mary said, than she began humming a tune, noticing that Christina was becoming upset.

The rest of the day was spent singing, and praying. Eating, and reading. Christina hung onto every word Mary and Joe had to offer about this book that her dad loved so much. Christina had decided that prayer was where all the power came from, but figured she would read more just to be sure. At bed time Christina was more tired than she could ever remember being. Her stomach was to full to get relaxed, but she finally faded off to sleep.

# [DREAM-TIME]

Christina's favorite dream came tonight. As she sat on the front porch swing, her beautiful little daughter played ball out in the front yard. Christina watched her as she chased the ball, and laughed and played.

{Christina always cherished the dream}

Christina was awakened by the crowing of roosters. It was still dark out but it was time to go.

Christina, BLACKWALL, and Big Red

**head toward Washington.**

# CHAPTER ELEVEN
## RENO NEVADA

*"What the hell happened here?"*

Christina asked, as if Big Red knew and was going to tell her everything.

*"I have seen this before."*

Christina said, recalling the dream that she had back at Mary and Joe's farm.

Everything was burnt or flattened, not one thing was left standing. The stench that filled the air burned Christina's eyes and noise.

*"Let's get the hell out of here."*

Christina said, as her skin crawled with cold goose bumps.

Christina turned BLACKWALL, than she leaned forward in the saddle. BLACKWALL lunged into an extremely fast run, like the gates of hell just opened up behind him. Big Red ran as fast as he could to keep up; after ten minutes Christina slowed BLACKWALL to a fast walk. Half a day later, the stench had began to fade from the air, BLACKWALL was breathing way too hard when Christina found a windmill that was in working condition.

*"The essence of life."*

Christina said, grabbing her binoculars and climbed up the latter that is attached to the side of the water-tower.

The landscape was not what Christina had envisioned, this landscape was barren, rocks and dry weeds covered the ground. Christina looks around in all directions; it seemed she could see forever, but nothing to be concerned about. She looked back toward the direction they had came from, then she spy's a white dot, maybe not it is gone now. Christina set camp and then gave BLACK-WALL his rub down as she whistled his favorite tune, and then she began the chore of cleaning and cooking the ground squirrels she had gathered throughout the day; ground squirrels are not very tasty, but they were plentiful in this part of the country. After dinner was finished, Christina had happy teardrops rolling down her cheeks as she set with Big Red's head lying across her feet with his ears perked up as she read her dad's book out loud through her watery eyes. Christina went to bed and faded off to sleep, perfectly content with her situation.

Christina woke up this morning with no Big Red in sight. She worried he was on another one of his dangerous missions as she packed camp. After she had camp all packed she saw Big Red slipping back into camp.

*"Now you show up; let's head north."*

Christina said, mounting BLACKWALL and heading in that direction.

The next two weeks were uneventful. She kept a steady pace to the northwest. Every so-often she would climb up a windmill to have a look around to make sure that there were no migrating U.N. DEMON'S. As Christina looks this evening, she spy's that white dot again. Christina focuses her binoculars.

*"What in the hell, a palomino. O.K I am not a skitso, someone is following us."*

Christina told herself, watching as the small palomino vanishes before her eyes.

Christina watches for a long time, whoever this person is seem excellent at camouflage; plus whoever this person is, it is a small person.

*"Maybe it's one of those Chinese people, they are suppose to be some kind of ninjas, having some kind of disappearing ability."*

Christina considers; as she starts her descent from the tower.

Christina stood between BLACKWALL and Big Red considering the situation, she decides that they will camp for the night. Whoever it is does not seem dangerous.

This-morning the sky was cloudy and the light breeze coming from the northwest made the morning feel even cooler than it really was. After Christina had camp all packed upon the back of BLACKWALL, she climbed the tower to scout the area. The palomino with the little person was nowhere in sight.

*"Damn you are good."*

Christina nervously giggled, slowly beginning her descent from the water tower.

*"We are going to ride a little fast today to see if the palomino can keep up."*

Christina said; she mounts BLACKWALL and started the days ride.

Christina slightly leans forward in the saddle, putting BLACKWALL into a fast trot. She spent the rest of day moving quickly, as if she was in a slight hurry but nothing life threatening.

Midday, Christina stopped for a lunch break. She took her binoculars and up a tree she went.

*"Where—are—you?"*

Christina asks precisely, as she began to scan back down the trail behind them.

*"There---you---are."*

Christina said proudly, spying the small palomino behind a group of large bushes.

*"Who, in the hell, are you?"*

Christina whispers, losing sight of the small pony.

The trees were more prevalent now in this part of the country. Christina was now entering a lush's forest landscape. Christina was thankful for that.

As daylight slipped away, Christina came up to a welcoming stream of water. She decided to camp for the night. She climbed a tall tree with binoculars in hand, and waits to see her stalker. Just as the stalker got into sight, the stalker turns toward the stream and disappears.

*"There you are, I see you're good at camouflage, and good at tracking, but who the hell are you and just what is it that you want."*

Christina pondered, climbing down the tall tree and then she begins to unsaddle BLACKWALL and give him his rub down.

After camp was set and the camp fire was ready, Christina retrieved her fishing line and hooks from the saddle and headed for the river. Big Red always enjoyed this event most, Christina would always sing when she was fishing. After dinner everyone settled into their sleeping aria.

## {DREAM-TIME} [ NIGHTMARE]

Christina stood at the bottom of a long hill looking up, she sees her sister Sera standing at the top; waving with a big smile.

*"There you are, I have been looking for you."*

Christina said, starting up the hill with a big smile on her face, happy to see her sister.

As Christina begins to climb up the slope, she hears a little girl screaming.

*"Over here – Over here! We must hide, NOW!!"*

The little girl was continuously screaming with fear in her voice and on her face.

She was waving her arms into the air as she stood at the entrance of a very large cave. Christina felt fear cascading throughout her body, as she watched her daughter pointing toward the cave.

### [CHRISTINA WAKES]

*"It's just a dream. ---- It's just a dream."*

Christina declared, as she concentrated on controlling her breathing and her body trembling.

Christina made today's ride an easy journey, slowly rambling along, Not too concerned about her stalker so much as she softly sang some tunes, but conflicting about dads book, and how Mary and Joe had said if you ask the right question, he will answer you.

"O.K. God, here's the deal. I'm asking to find Sera."

Christina said, wondering if she was doing it right.

*"Ask and you shall receive, also, He that lacks knowledge let him ask, the father will give it freely."*

Christina meditated on those passages a few moments, as she repeated them out loud.

*"THAT'S IT!! All I have to do is ask God to give me knowledge of what the book is saying."*

Christina shouted loudly, sitting up high in the saddle, as if she had just discovered all the secrets to the universe.

Big Red, approached running from up the trail. He stops in front of Christina, giving one of his famous deep down air puffs than he looked up at Christina.

*"You have got ~ to be shitting me, more U. N. DEMON'S, O.K. you pick the direction."*

Christina said, as she set and looked up the trail.

Big red gave a loud bark, and headed back down the trail like he understood what she had said.

*"There is someone that way to."*

Christina said, turning herself in the saddle to get a look at Big Red's back side.

Big Red gave another loud bark, keeping his sturdy trot down the trail.

*"I guess we are going to meet the china man today."*

Christina whispered; turning BLACKWALL and following Big Red.

A little ways down the trail, Big Red made a right turn into the stream and then swam over to the other side. Christina and BLACKWALL follows.

*"Have I ever told you, that you are the best damn dog that I have ever met?"*

Christina bolstered, as she was riding out of the stream onto dry land.

Big Red stayed in the lead throughout the day. As the evening crept closer he brought them back to the river a little bit further to the north of the DEMON'S.

Christina set camp, cooked dinner, and then she waited until it was dark. She climbed a tree to take herself a look down the river. She could see the reflection of a small fire glistening off the water a couple of miles away.

"Son- of- a- bitch. Who, in the hell, are you?"

Christina wondered to herself, slowly climbing down the tree.

Christina's sleep was restless tonight, but she finally faded off to sleep.

This morning when Christina awakens, she does not see Big Red. She rose up and looked all around, no Big Red.

"Where in the hell is Big Red?"

Christina shouts, even though there is no one around to give an answer; she begins packing up the camp.

After BLACKWALL was all packed and ready to go, Big Red slithered back into camp.

*"You're not much of a watch dog, where you been?"*

Christina scolded, as she stared down at Big Red with a disappointing look.

Big Red gave a small bark and went and laid down in the shade to wait for Christina.

Their journey begins today with sunshine and a slight breeze, Christina's mind kept wondering back to her stalker. He was always just far enough away that she could never get a descent look at him.

*"I need a plan."*

Christina said, as her mind slipped into gear on devising herself a plan.

The plan that she concocted consisted of her grabbing onto a low lying tree limb and then shimmering down the tree and hide. Then lay and wait for her stalker to pass by. Christina knew that BLACKWALL was good at this game. He would keep going until he was out of her sight, and then he would wait for her all clear whistle. She had figured the stalker would most likely continue to keep his eyes fixed on BLACKWALL'S tracks.

*"Sounds good on paper, so, here we go."*

Christina said, spotting a low limb hanging across the trail, and then she implemented her plan.

The tree bark was a bit rougher on her skin than she cared for, but BLACKWALL was out of sight and she was on the ground. Christina found a group of thick bushes; she ducks in behind them to wait. Big Red came and imposed himself into her space as he lay down and went to sleep.

*"See how you are."*

Christina said with sarcasm in her voice, as she situated herself so to get a good view.

About an hour into her stake-out, she hears the sound of the palomino and the stalker coming up the trail. Christina sits up with intensity in her bones, and then realizes she had not made a plan for the actual catching of the stalker. The stalker passed under the limb that Christina had used; instantly the stalker turned in retreat as if Satan himself had reached-up from beneath the ground and tried to grab them. The palomino's retreat was one big dramatic experience. The small palomino was giving everything that it had in order to satisfy his owner. Christina set entranced in complete shock as the look of terror on the stalkers face was etched into her mind forever. She looked over at Big Red who had laid back down. She stared at him with suspicion, and then she reaches over and slaps Big Red on the butt, hard. Big Red jumps straight up with a loud squawk, unsuspecting of the punishment Christina imposed up on him.

*"YOU KNEW!!! --- YOU KNEW!!!"*

Christina exclaimed, as she rose-up, staring down the trail in the direction that the palomino had made its escape.

*"That is where you have been going, when I wake up early and you are not here, that is where you have been going."*

Christina accused Big Red, slowly walking out onto the trail with Big Red following.

Christina whistles for BLACKWALL, and then she continued staring down the trail, as she stood between BLACKWALL and Big Red, considering this to be a unexpected disturbing and concerning situation.

*"It's a child, ---- It's just a damn child."*

Christina said, looking down at Big Red, with watery eyes.

Big Red is completely confused.

*"What are we going to do, Big Red? It's just a small child."*

Christina whispered, as tears began to seep out from her eyes as she stared at Big Red.

Big Red, watched in confusion, he'd never seen Christina act this way before.

*"I know what we are going to do. We'll pitch camp right here, until that child comes back."*

Christina said, with authority, as she begins to unsaddle BLACKWALL in the center of trail.

# CHAPTER TWELVE
## [CHRISTINA'S DAUGHTER]

The palomino was squeezing out every bit of energy it had in order to satisfy his owner's demands. He had begun to breathe too hard. Sera pulled back on the range and slowed Crazy Horse to a walk. She glanced back up over her shoulder still trembling from the frightening experience.

*"The giant should have caught us by now."*

Sera told Crazy Horse between gasp of air, she turned Crazy Horse to a stop, and then stared back up the trail expecting to see a black beast coming down the trail any second.

Sera, is a twelve year old girl, four feet tall, when she stood up straight; with big brown eyes, and long black hair. 90 lb. soaking wet. Sera's mother died during her birth; Sera had been raised by her grandfather, but he had died in his sleep about thirteen months ago. Her father had been killed by U.N. DEMON'S before she was born. Sera, is completely all on her own now.

Sera listened intensively, focusing her ears as hard as she possibly could to separate out the sound of Crazy Horse's breathing, and her heart pounding in her chest, and the sound of a giant's monster black beast. Sera knew there was no way for Crazy Horse to out run the beast that the giant rode. Sera slipped down from Crazy Horse, she leads him behind the tiny group of short trees. Being small has a lot of advantages, and Sera knew how to exploit every single one of them.

*"Where is she?"*

Sera asked Crazy Horse, as she reaches for her binoculars.

Sera pulled the strap up over her head as she begins to climb up the tallest tree she can find and still keeping close to Crazy Horse, trying to figure out where the giant is at.

*"This makes no since at all."*

Sera whispered, as she watches Christina set up camp right in the middle of the trail.

*"Doesn't she know how dangerous it is to be out in the open like that? But her tent is so cool."*

Sera said to Crazy Horse, slowly climbing down the tree, feeling a little bit relieved that the giant was not coming after her.

With her anxiety's beginning to calm, Sera begins to set her camp up. The dreary thoughts of being lonely seemed to diminish the fears that she may have about the giant.

Christina sets camp as Big Red sat up under a tree, still confused as to why she was so upset. He liked the small person; the small ones seemed to be more playful than the big ones.

*"How do you approach a small child?"*

Christina pondered, as she set with her back up against her saddle, with her father's book and her binoculars.

Christina caught a strong scent of wild pigs in the air.

*"That's it, roasted pork."*

Christina shouted, jumping to her feet.

Christina quickly retrieved her three piece throw spear and her hunting knife from the pile of supplies and disappeared into the woods as she was putting the spear together, with the thought of roasting pork fragrance that would soon be filling the air. She was careful to keep down-wind of the wild boar as she closed in on their position. The wild boar did not seem to be bothered with her presence. Christina threw her spear and quickly climbed a tree, just as Rosie had taught her to do. She patently waited for the turmoil to subside and then she climbed down the tree and claimed her prize. When Christina returned from the hunt, she was carrying the hind quarter of a fat pig. She built a gigantic camp fire so to make sure that the tiny child would be able to see the flames clearly. Then she set the hind quarter of pork onto the pit.

"Giants must have very small brains."

Sera concluded, clearly watching as the large flames from the fire were leaping into the sky.

"O. K. I know that she is not a real giant, but gees she is Soooo, big."

Sera whispers to Crazy horse, as she begins to catch the fragrance of roasting pork in the air.

Sera drifted off to sleep with the thoughts of her grandfather standing over an open fire pit, cooking dinner for the two of them.

# {SERA'S DREAM}

Sera's favorite dream comes tonight. The one with the mom she never had. They were in a big garden with all kinds of vegetables, picking tomatoes. Then Sera would shout, "food fight," and she and mom would throw tomatoes at each other as they laughed and played in the garden.

Sera woke up with a tremendous smile on her face. She often wondered at the blond hair, and blue eyes her mom had. But she always relished the dream.

## [CHRISTINA'S DREAM]

Christina's favorite dream came tonight. As she was preparing dinner, her beautiful daughter sat at the table.

"Mom, I'm hungry, how much longer? I'm starving."

Christina's daughter asked, walking over beside Christina and looking at the roast.

"Pork can only cook so fast. You must learn to have patients."

Christina explained, leaning down to give her a hug.

"Can I have a tomato while I wait?"

Her daughter asked in a whiny voice, than she hugged Christina as hard as she could.

"Yes, you may."

Christina said, as she gave her a ripe red tomato.

Sera and Christina woke up this morning to the strong aroma of the roasting pork filling the air. They both climbed out from their tents and retrieved their binoculars. Sera's stomach was growling loudly as she climbed the tree to get a good look toward the giant's camp. With all the excitement yesterday, Sera had not had the time to hunt for dinner.

*"God, I'm starving."*

Sera whispered, settling down into a place in the tree.

Sera focused her binoculars up toward the giant's camp, with her mouth watering from the aroma of roasting pork.

*"She can see me!"*

Sera exclaimed, as she jolted backward in the tree, attempting to hide behind a small limb.

Christina was standing in plain sight beside the fire as she watched Sera through her binoculars. Christina watched Sera climb the tree, and found a little humor as she was watching Sera's attempt to hide behind the small limb. Sera looked cute slowly peeked around the small limb, than through her binoculars. She could see Christina standing with her binoculars looking back toward her. Christina seemed to be making some hand motions toward the fire pit, where the smoking pork-roast was cooking.

"Gees, I am so hungry."

Sera whispered, deciding that for a taste of fresh cooked pork, she would embrace the danger of meeting the giant.

Christina watched the tiny figure as she climbed down the tree, and then starts to pack camp onto the back of the palomino.

"I think she's coming."

Christina said with excitement in her voice, as she continued looking through her binoculars.

"What if she doesn't like me, "MY GOD" What if she does. What in the hell are we going to do with a small child?"

Christina asked, taking a quick look down at Big Red with a worried look on her face.

Christina talked to herself, as she paced to and fro across the camp, constantly stopping to look and check on the girl's progress.

"Come on damn it, can't your horse run?"

Christina inquired, as she anticipates on the girl's arrival.

"I don't know about this."

Sera said, as she slowed to a crawl, than she brought Crazy horse to a stop.

She was about 50 yards away, when she focused on the giant, not 100%, devoting to the situation. Big Red noticed the hesitation, so he jumps up and runs to Sera with enthusiasm. Big Red darted around and around Crazy Horse and Sera. Sera slip's off Crazy Horse than gives Big Red a tight squeeze around his neck. Christina has never seen Big Red acting this way before. She watches in amazement as the two seemed to be best of friends.

"Gees Red, she is really big."

Sera whispered to Big Red, as she rose up and looked toward Christina.

Big Red gently puts Sera's hand inside his mouth and then he slowly begins to walk towards Christina. Christina stands in place, frozen, like she was a statue. Sera stops ten feet away.

{IT'S A DAVID AND GOLIATH MOMENT}

"4 feet -V- 5 feet 11 inches."

They stare in amassment at the size of the other, taking in every square inch of each other's features. Christina noticed how much Sera looks like the girl in her dreams, with long straight coal black hair and sparkling brown eyes; as Sera has noticed how much Christina look like her dream mom, with long wavy blond hair and sky blue eyes. Christina broke the silence.

"Hi, my name is Christina."

Christina said, with a soft voice and friendly smile; trying her best not to be intimidating to the tiny frame that was standing in front of her.

"Hi......I'm.....Sera."

Sera said, trying her very best to control the trembling in her voice; knowing this giant of a woman could easily crush her.

Christina felt a fusion of sensations running through her body when she heard the name Sera, echoing through her head.

"Are... you...O.K.?"

Sera ask, becoming concerned about the look on Christina's face.

"Yes...Yes...Are you hungry?"

Christina answered, as she tried to regain a little bit of her focus.

*"Yes, please."*

Sera said, as her stomach gave a loud and deep recognizable growl.

*"Great, let's eat."*

Christina said, turning and then starts toward the fire pit where the appetizing meal awaits.

Christina cut large portions of meat for each of them, putting it onto tin plates. Pork is a real treat these days and times. Sera already had her big hunting knife ready, as she took the plate from Christina. They both set and ate in silence, with only the sound of smacking lips enjoying the tasty meal. When they had their fill, Christina leaned back up against her saddle and Sera lay back against Big Red and then began to relax.

*"That was, fan~tastic."*

Sera said, laying her head back against Big Red, looking up and staring at the fluffy popcorn clouds that were floating by.

*"Thank you."*

Christina said, feeling a little gratitude of satisfaction knowing she has made a new friend today.

*"This is not a very good situation."*

Sera inform Christina, slowly turning to look her in the eyes.

"What do you mean?"

Christina asks, with a wary look on her face, and worry present in her voice.

"We are way too full, and this is now a dangerous place to be."

Sera said, setting up looking straight in to Christina's eyes.

"Because~ I had a big fire and cooked a lot of meat and now every wild animal and radicals can smell it all."

Christina said, as she rose up and started to take inventory of their situation.

"Exactly right."

Sera said, standing up, and then started to walk towards Crazy Horse.

"I'm going northwest to Washington, so maybe you will join me."

Christina said, quickly walking toward Sera and Crazy horse.

"YES!! I mean, no one is waiting at home for me, so I would love to."

Sera exclaimed, looking at Christina with a twinkle in her eyes, and a tremendous smile upon her face.

"*Great, let's ride.*"

Christina said, as she quickly started to pack camp onto BLACKWALL.

Christina and Sera were excited to be off on their new adventures that they would be making together. They both were filled with a variety of emotions, as they began to recall all their dreams that they have had of each other as they rode along. Midday they decided it was time to take a short break.

"*Christina, do you have family?*"

Sera ask, all excited about having another human to speak with.

"*Yes, I have an older sister that I'm looking for, how about you.*"

Christina ask, as curiosity about why such a small child would be out here all alone, weighed heavy on her mind.

"*NOPE, all dead.*"

Sera said point blank, looking down and turning her eyes away from Christina's eyes.

"*O.K. How long has your mother been gone?*"

Christina asks, putting her hand on Sera's back and gently began to rub.

"*My mom died before I was born, so my grandpapa raised me.*"

Sera said, and then she leaned back up against Christina's hand, enjoying the gentle rub.

"Wait.--- Wait.-- How can she die, before you were born?"

Christina asks, as her forehead had begun to wrinkle from confusion.

"Grandpapa said, one minute after she died, then he cut me out."

Sera explained, raising her arm up and making a slashing motion as if she was holding a knife.

"WOW.—I mean... I can't....Just,... WOW."

Christina said; she was lost for the words to express her emotions.

"Yea,... I know, and my daddy was killed by those U.N. people, before I was born."

Sera said, drawing in a deep breath as she summoned up her enter strength she possessed.

"And your grandpapa?"

Christina softly asks, looking out in to space, still trying to processing everything Sera had just said.

"He just didn't wake up one day; that was about a year ago."

Sera said, with water clearly present in her eyes as she started fidgeting.

"*How old are you, sweetheart?*"

Christina asks, changing the subject; she could see the emotions that were building in Sera's eyes.

Sera turned and looked at Christina with a tear slowly drifting down her cheek. No one has ever called her sweetheart before, except for her dream mom.

"*Are you O. K.?*"

Christina asks, feeling the moister building up in her own eyes.

"*Yes.—Yes.- just no one ever call me that before; and I am twelve years old.*"

Sera said proudly, holding her head up high as she stood up.

"*Wow twelve, you look around seven or eight.*"

Christina expressed, studying Sera's features a little more closely.

"*Yea,.. I know, I look good for my age.*"

Sera said, with humor in her voice as she began to giggle.

Christina could not help but to laugh at the sarcasm, both started laughing with each other as they mounted up, than continued on their long journey. The day was sunny, warm, and breezy. A perfect day for riding, Christina and Sera rode side by side.

*"Christina."*

Sera said in a question form, as she stared straight ahead.

*"Yes, sweetheart, what is it?"*

Christina asked, looking over and giving a serious smile to Sera.

*"If I let you continue calling me sweetheart, then I get to call you, MOM. Deal?"*

Sera ask with anticipation in her voice, as she turned to see Christina's reaction.

BLACKWALL came to a complete stop, and gave out a loud nay, as he felt the surge of shock going through Christina's body. Sera pulled Crazy Horse to a stop as she turned in the saddle to look back at Christina. Big Red gave a loud bark.

*"Yes,... Yes sweetheart, you may."*

Christina said with pride in her voice, than began to move BLACKWALL forward, feeling a warm sensation through her body.

The rest of the day Sera would say, mom, just to hear the word and to feel it upon her lips. Christina would smile and say, my little sweet- heart. As the sun drew close to the horizon, they came up on a small river. It was about 20 ft. wide and 4 ft. deep.

*"We will camp here tonight."*

Christina said, as she dismounted and took a look around.

*"Sounds good to me, mom."*

Sera said, not missing any chance that she could find to call Christina, mom.

Sera slid down off Crazy Horse and began to set camp. After camp was set, Sera retrieved her binoculars and started toward a tall tree.

*"I got this."*

Sera said, desperately wanting to prove she could take care of herself.

*"She is too damn young, for this shit."*

Christina said, watching Sera walking away with her binoculars.

The fish for dinner was delicious; the bath in the cool river was fantastic; the small fire to warm up by was perfect. Christina took the hair brush from Sera's small hand, and slowly began to brush Sera's long black hair from behind.

*"God, that feels so good."*

Sera said, closing her eyes and embracing the feeling of having a mom.

There was just enough light left, to read a little of dad's book. Sera listened with intensity, as she ran her hand over Big Red.

"Interesting book, who is it about?"

Sera asked; watching Christina putting the book back into the leather bag.

"The son of God."

Christina answers, reaching over and gently pushing Sera's hair behind her ear.

"WHAT ! I didn't know God had a son."

Sera proclaimed, reaching over and gently pushed Christina's hair behind her ear.

"Yes, sweetheart, he did."

Christina said, as she put some more wood onto the fire.

"Is it hard to read?"

Sera ask in a serious voice, staring into the flames.

"Are you saying, you can't read?"

Christina asks with surprise in her voice, and on her face.

"NOPE, and neither could grandpapa."

Sera said, keeping her eyes trained on the fire.

"I can teach you, if you would like."

Christina said, than she put her arm around Sera's shoulder.

"YES !! Thank you mom, thank you so, so much."

Sera said with enthusiasm, wrapping her arms around Christina and giving her a squeeze.

Christina and Sera set by the small fire, Christina's arms wrapped around Sera, and Sera leaning up against Christina, slowly fading into dream land as Christina sang a lullaby to her.

"Were you named after your mom?"

Sera softly asked, leaning up against Christina and watching her feet wiggle in the flickering light from the fire.

"No sweetheart, after my grandmother."

Christina said, gently laying her head down on top of Sera's head.

"Grandpapa named me after my mother."

Sera said, wrapping her fingers into the fingers of Christina's hand.

*"You look like you're American Indian, was your mother also an Indian?"*

Christina asks, beginning to gently rock Sera to and fro.

*"No, grandpapa said she was white, but dad was Indian."*

Sera said, her voice began to fade and her feet stopped wiggling.

*"How long did your mom and dad know each other?"*

Christina quietly asked, attempting to keep Sera distracted from her slow drift into sleep.

*"Not long; Mom was from, pepsi--vina."*

Sera said, her eyes began to get heavy and drift closed.

Christina sat and thought about what she said for a few minutes.

*"You mean, Pennsylvania."*

Christina said, as she stopped rocking than raised her head up off of Sera's.

*"Yea, that sounds right."*

Sera mumbled, as her body went limp lying up against Christina.

*"Sera, sweetheart, I need you to wake up."*

Christina said; she gently shook Sera with the arm she had around her shoulder.

*"What's wrong?—What's up?"*

Sera said, her head immediately lifting as she became aware of her surroundings.

*"This is very important, O. K. do you know how old your mother would have been when you were born?"*

Christina asks, with a tremble in her voice as she began to shake a little.

*"Yea,- she was twenty two, she was too young to die, that's what grandpapa said.,"*

Sera said, with aggravation in her voice for being woken up.

*"Do you know if she worked anywhere?"*

Christina asks with anxiety in her voice, and she began to noticeably shake.

*"Grandpapa said she was a U.S. police, why?"*

Sera answered, slowly beginning to sit-up straight, growing concerned about all of the interrogation.

Christina set, with tears starting to spill out of her eyes. Sera stood and moved around into the front of Christina, and put her hands on each side of Christina's face.

*"O.K.- I'm not a stupid little girl, what's up?"*

Sera demanded an immediate answer to her question from Christina.

Christina took a deep breath, as she wiped her eyes; she gently took Sera by the hand and then looked into her eyes.

*"O. K.- My sister is white, she would have been twenty two when you were born, and her name is Sera."*

Christina had to stop and regroup, taking in another deep shaky breath as Sera stared into her eyes.

**"Was she a U.S. police!?"**

Sera demanded, as she herself had begun to tremble and tears ran down her cheeks.

*"Yes,- Yes she was."*

Christina whispered, as tears ran freely from her eyes.

*"I have a picture of my mother, I have a picture, I will go and get it."*

Sera exclaimed, jumping up and running fast, as fast as her tiny legs could go toward her saddle bags.

Christina put more wood onto the fire so to give more light, as Sera began digging into her saddle bag.

*"I found it, I got it."*

Sera yelled, waving the picture around in the air, running back toward Christina.

Christina waited patiently as Sera slowly and carefully un-wrapped the picture from its water proof packet, and then held it up to the light.

*"My sister, Sera."*

Christina whispered, softly drifting her finger across the picture.

Christina and Sera, set in front of the fire as they held onto each other, crying and then laughing, and then crying together.

Sera, was the first to speak.

*"Mom, I think I really,- really need you to sleep in my tent with me tonight."*

Sera said, squeezing as hard as her little arms could possibly squeeze.

*"You know what. I think I need that too."*

Christina said, gently rocking Sera.

# CHAPTER THIRTEEN
## BONDING TIME

Morning came with a slight chill in the air. Sera wakes up alone in her tent, she climbs out and looked around as she stretches. Big Red lay next to the fire, the horses stood under a tree. Crazy Horse looks like a tiny little toy next to BLACKWALL. Sera slowly walked down to the river to wash up, she always loves the days when there was water to rinse off in. Sera was walking back toward the camp fire, when she noticed Christina coming down the trail from the woods with her binoculars in her hand. Sera ran straight into Christina's arms.

*"I love you so much, mom."*

Sera said, squeezing Christina as hard as she could, filled with a joy like she had never known.

*"And I love you so very much, my beautiful little daughter."*

Christina proclaimed, hugging Sera as tightly as she dared.

Christina and Sera set by the fire, both lost in the moment of mother & daughter emotions, as Christina set behind Sera braiding her hair into pony tails.

*"Time to make a new plan."*

Christina said, continuing to carefully braid Sera's long black hair.

*"I'm sorry mother died."*

Sera said sadly, savoring every tiny touch with her eyes closed.

*"Me to, but now I have you, and I have always wanted and dreamed of having a daughter."*

Christina said, tying the ends of sera's pony tails together.

*"And I have always dreamed of having a great mom."*

Sera said, reaching back and taking one of Christina's hands for a moment.

*"I see no reason for us to keep going north. It's beginning to get damn cold up there."*

Christina said, standing and turning Sera towards her to examine her handy work.

*"So, are we going back to New Mexico?"*

Sera ask, swinging her head side to side so that the pony tails would plop around.

*"Wait,--what do you mean back, when were you in New Mexico?"*

Christina asks, trying to keep from laughing at Sera swinging her head around.

Sera gave her an answer as she and Christina began to pack up camp.

*"I started following you back when you left that farm."*

Sera said, as she begins to fasten things to the back of Crazy Horse.

*"No way,--- No way you followed me that far without me seeing you."*

Christina countered, fastening camp on to the back of BLACKWALL.

*"I'm good, grandpapa was a good teacher."*

Sera proclaimed, waiting for Christina to finish packing.

*"Yes you are .O.K. We will head south to Arizona then east to New Mexico."*

Christina said, putting her foot in the stirrup and mounts BLACKWALL.

*"Let's ride."*

Sera said, mounting Crazy Horse and then began to ride south.

This day was a nice day, not too hot not too cold. Christina starts to sing songs that Mary and Joe had taught her. She was amazed that Sera could hear her sing a song one time and she would remember every word and to the song. Sera was constantly curious, listened with intensity to everything that Christina was teaching her. It reminded Christina about her teenage years, and how Rosie had taught her back then. The day pasted quickly. After they settled on a place to camp, Christina and Sera climbed a tall tree with their binoculars in hand. This was the most fun part of the day, and they both liked being way up high looking out far beyond what the imagination could imagine. Christina was beginning to teach Sera how to read using her dad's book. Then she would use a clear spot on the ground to teach her math. Sera seem to have this ability to remember everything that she would see, never forgetting. Christina was amazed at Sera's ability. Christina and Sera have complete devotion to their mother daughter relationship. They had grown to love and care deeply for each other. If the nights were warm and clear and calm they would share their net tent, if the night was cold and rainy, then they would share their solid tent. Considering the devastation of today's world, they were living a good life.

The flames flickered in the night air as Sera sets facing the fire with Christina brushed her long hair.

"*Mom, will you tell me about my mother?*"

Sera ask, relishing in the sensation of the tender feeling of Christina brushing her hair.

*"Yes, of course I will sweetheart."*

Christina said, than she began to put Sera's hair up into pony tails.

Christina started, with the horse ranch that her family had long ago. Then the sand castles that she and Sera her sister had built at the beach house.

Christina and Sera have been riding hard to stay out in front of the cold weather coming down from the north. They are now entering northern Arizona. This part of Arizona is a mountainous region with a lush green forest, and the nights can become extremely cold this time of the year, even though the days get nice and warm. They agreed to set camp early in order to have the time to build a fire for the night. They found a cave about the size of a three bedroom house. But the cave stank to bad to use for sleeping. They set camp a short ways away.

Christina went to hunt for the day's dinner as Sera built the fire pit. Sera had just finished with the pit when Big Red came running from the north at top speed. When he reaches Sera, he stopped, and then he gave one of his deep down whisper air barks, staring up at Sera.

*"What is wrong? Is it mom? Is she hurt?"*

Sera ask, looking all around for any sign of Christina.

Big Red ran to the cave then gave a deep loud bark and ran back to Sera, then to the cave. Sera began to tremble. She realized what it was that Big Red wanted. He wanted her to go and hide inside the cave. Big Red stood at the cave waiting impatiently for Sera. Her adrenaline was pumping extra hard, the saddles felt light as feathers. She packed camp onto BLACKWALL.

*"Let's go!"*

Sera shouted, when she started moving in the direction of the cave.

With the horse's safe inside the cave, Sera turns her concern back to Christina.

*"MOM! – I have to go find mom."*

Sera said, heading toward the entrance.

Big Red stood at the entrance of the cave with his head down and staring straight at Sera. Big Red showed his k-9 teeth and gave a loud growl, blocking the way out of the cave.

*"O. K.—O. K.- We'll wait."*

Sera conceited; turning and retrieving her binoculars from her saddle bag.

Sera and Big Red sat at the entrance of the cave, she could see smoke rising up through the trees to the north. The smoke was close enough to see without binoculars. Sera set franticly looking for Christina through her binoculars. She saw her mom coming from the south. She stood up beside Big Red, waiting impatiently.

Christina walked into the camp without an inclination to the trouble. She felt her heart begin to pound. She noticed the camp was empty. She franticly looked around for Sera.

*"OVER HERE! OVER HERE! We have to hide now."*

Sera scream's at Christina, waving her arms into the air.

Christina looked up the hill to see Sera with her arms waving franticly into the air. Her mind went back to her nightmare that she had back at the farm. She quickly runs up the hill to Sera.

*"SHIT! SHIT! SHIT!"*

Christina said, standing beside Sera and Big Red at the entrance of the cave.

Christina knew that Crazy horse could not run faster than the U.N. DEMON'S horses, especially if their horses were good ones. She considered their situation as she looked north, through her binoculars.

*"We have no choice, but to hide in here."*

Christina said, gathering up their bow and arrows and throw spears and puts them by the entrance.

*"I have never killed anyone before."*

Sera said, as she'd begun trembling, and a tear rolled down her cheek.

*"To be perfectly honest sweetheart, I've never killed anyone before ether."*

Christina said, wrapping Sera in her arms and holding her tight.

Christina knows that they are now at a disadvantage, especially if the U.N. DEMON'S discover their hiding place.

Big Red lowers his head, then gives a loud deep growl as he stares up at Christina.

*"What's up with you?"*

Christina asked, turning her attention to Big Red.

*"He wants us to go inside, that's what he did to me earlier, when he wouldn't let me out of the cave to go and find you."*

Sera said, taking hold of Christina's arm, then pulled her deep into the cave.

Christina and Sera, quietly set in the cave listening, as Big Red sat half-way outside the entrance.

"*I think I found them.*"

Christina hears a man's deep loud voice, with a foreign ascent echoing through the cave.

"*Comrade, Comrade, Come on out of the hole. Maybe I let you live.*"

The man yelled loudly, as he spoke with his German accent.

"*We are going to have to kill these men Sera, if we don't, they will kill us.*"

Christina said, with tears started to run down her cheeks.

"*NO!*"

Sera quietly shouted, as she deeply buries her face into Christina's bosom.

"*We have no choice baby girl.*"

Christina said somberly, and then she wrapped her arms around Sera.

"*NO!- All we have to do is keep them outside, until tomorrow morning.*"

Sera said with a muzzled voice, forcing her face deeper into Christina.

"*And tomorrow will change things, how?*"

Christina asks, softly rubbing her hands over Sera's hair.

"*Dad will be here tomorrow morning.*"

Sera said point blank, than she raised her head and looked up at Christina.

"*I love you sweetheart, but my dad and your dad, are both dead, so I don't think they are coming.*"

Christina said, gently wiping the tears from Sera's eyes.

"*Don't be silly mom, I mean my new dad. I had this exact dream, my new daddy always came to save me.*"

Sera said, than she returned her face into Christina's body, squeezing with trembling arms.

"*I had this same dream myself. We'll wait for your new dad.*"

Christina said, reaching down then slowly lifting Sera into her arms.

"*Son-of-a-bitch, they have a guard dog.*"

A man's voice yelled, as he noticed Big Red standing in the entrance.

Big Red was standing with his ears and tail and the hair on his back, straight up. He gave a cold, hard stare, down on the U.N.DEMON'S.

Christina set Sera down than pointed to the back of the cave. Then she turns and walked over to the entrance of the cave, she stood tall, all five ft. eleven in. next to Big Red.

*"I do have weapons, and I am prepared to use them."*

Christina said, looking down at the men and counts eight U. N. DEMON'S.

*"I got to get me some of that."*

One of the men said, with a deep German accent.

Christina stands and watches in fear, as the DEMON'S whoop and yell with laughter.

*"I will give you until tomorrow morning to reconsider, and then I am going to burn you out."*

The man yelled, and then he turned and began to unpack his horse.

Christina turned and walked back into the cave to where Sera set waiting.

*"You, stay out of sight."*

Christina said; she considered what those men would do to a beautiful little girl if they were to find her.

*"I know mom, I'm not stupid."*

Sera said, knowing the consequences of them finding her.

Christina set down beside Sera, than leaned her back against the wall and took a deep shaky breath as she tried to control her trembling. Sera crawled into Christina's lap and buried herself into Christina, than she begins to uncontrollably sob. Christina gently rocks her back and forth, as she desperately searches her mind in the hope she can figure a way out of their situation.

# CHAPTER FOURTEEN
## MY NEW DAD

Christina set, with Sera sleeping on her lap. Throughout the night she would occasionally doze off for a moment, from time to time, but she mostly stayed awake.

Big Red sat at the entrance, keeping alert all night, watching the U. N. DEMON'S with keen eyes and ears.

Christina was getting plenty of practice on her praying skills. She'd pray for a miracle. Then she prayed for deliverance. She was praying really hard, that Sera's mythical dad would come save the day. Then she prayed for God's power to protect Sera.

*"GOD.- No matter what, please protect Sera."*

Christina prayed; with Sera asleep in her lap as tears rolled down her cheeks.

The sun peeked above the horizon and Sera began to stir, Christina had all the essentials to insure Sera's survival, packed and put onto BLACKWALL. Christina set Sera in her lap than held her face in her hands.

*"Listen to me very carefully. You will have to hold on tight, as tight as you possibly can when BLACKWALL starts to run. He's very powerful and very fast. Do not~ listen to me, do not~ look back. You run as fast as you can, do not look back. We will meet at the farm house."*

Christina explained to Sera, trying her best to control the trembling in her voice, with her tears streaming down her face.

Sera held onto Christina for dear life, as she buried her head against Christina's body, nodding with a cry she could not control.

Christina picked Sera up and gave her a tight squeeze, and then she set her upon the back of BLACKWALL. Sera's small skinny body seemed to vanish into BLACKWALL'S massive frame.

*"I love you, my little sweetheart."*

Christina said, through the tears that were streaming down her face.

*"I will always love you mom."*

Sera said, as she takes hold of the front of the saddle, and then wrapped her legs tightly around BLACKWALL, preparing for the rush from the massive pile of muscle that she was sitting on.

As Christina prepares to release her hold on BLACKWALL, an extremely loud thunder echo's through the cave. Christina and BLACKWALL, jump at the sound.

*"What the hell was that?!!"*

Christina shouted, taking hold of the bridle while rubbing BLACKWALL'S neck.

Big Red stood at attention, staring out the entrance. Another extreme thunder roars through the cave.

*"Get down, sweetheart, hurry."*

Christina said, holding tightly to the bridle.

Christina took Sera off BLACKWALL. He had began to prance around, spooked by the loud noise. Christina rubbed his neck, than whistled a tune that he liked, so to settle him down. Christina cautiously walks to the entrance of the cave with Sera on her hills. She looked outside to see eight DEMON'S, riding franticly to the north. Fifty feet from where Christina stood, sat a fine specimen of a man, he looked to be in his early to mid thirty's, six ft. two in tall, 250 lb. blond hair, blue eyes, and with shoulders wide enough, to completely fill up a door way. The sight of this man, sitting on a gigantic gray mar, with this long gun in his hand, made Christina's knees grow weaker than they already were if that was even possible.

Sera darted out past Christina, as Christina stood completely entranced by this gorgeous man. He secured his gun back into its holder, and gracefully dismounted, and then watched this tiny girl running toward him.

*"I knew you would be here daddy, I just knew you would be here."*

Sera shouted, as she reached the man and put him into a tight embrace.

The man looked at Christina with a curious look upon his face, as Christina reaches and pulls Sera's arms out from around the man, than slowly takes a few steps back.

*"My name is Mike, are you ladies alright?"*

Mike asks, with a cute grin on his lips as he notices Christina's beauty.

Christina picked up Sera like she was her five years old little girl.

*"I'm not sure, are we?"*

Christina asks, holding tightly onto Sera, like she might try to get away.

*"I promise you are perfectly safe with me. My mom would skin me alive."*

Mike said, mystified, by the beauty of this lovely lady standing in front of him.

*"I'm sorry about Sera. It's just that we thought—well we thought this was it for us."*

Christina said, doing her best to look as if she was in complete control.

*"We need to go get our horses."*

Sera informed; squirming in the attempt to escape from Christina's grip that she had on her.

Christina set Sera down and took her hand, then started toward the cave.

*"Don't you go anywhere."*

Sera demanded, as Christina quickly pulled her toward the cave.

*"Sera, let's not call him daddy, we wouldn't want to scare him off."*

Christina said, as they reached the entrance of the cave.

*"Did you see how big he is, he's even bigger than you are."*

Sera said with excitement in her voice, as she followed Christina into the cave.

*"Yes sweetheart, I defiantly noticed."*

Christina said, with her face turning to a deep red with a sensation that she never knew existed and she has never experienced before.

"*I'm being silly, aren't I?*"

Sera said, following Christina out from the cave with Crazy horse in tow.

"*You are twelve years old. You are suppose to be a little silly.*"

Christina informs Sera, as they exited the cave, where Mike was waiting.

"*Your right, and he will be the best dad ever.*"

Sera said quickly, in a quiet voice as if she was sharing a secret with Christina.

Mike was still amazed at the beauty of this tall woman as he watched her and the tiny girl coming out of the cave with their horses that matched their sizes in tow.

"*I'm sorry that I didn't introduce myself, I am Christina.*"

Christina said to Mike, as they repacked all of their things onto the right horse.

"*Christina,- Beautiful,......I like that name.*"

Mike said, giving his cute smile and his wink, with his baby blue eyes.

*"Did he say I am beautiful, or my name is?"*

Christina though to herself, her stomach began to flutter with another sensation that was a first for her.

Big Red gave a bark to say, don't forget me.

*"O Yes, this is Big Red."*

Christina said, reaching down, giving him a pat on the head.

After everything was packed back on the right horse, Sera mounted Crazy Horse and she quickly began to speak.

*"O.-K.- Mike, we are headed east, over to New Mexico, So Maybe you can come with us."*

Sera said, with anticipation in her voice as her head bobbed up and down in a yes motion.

Christina gives Sera a look that says, {what in the hell are you doing}. Sera just gave her a huge smile, and shrugged her shoulders.

*"I am going east for a few days, but we will leave it up to your mother."*

Mike said with a chuckle, watching Sera's head bobbing up and down.

*"Not a problem."*

Christina said with just a touch of sarcasm, as she puts her foot into the stirrup and mounts BLACKWALL.

The day had become cloudy but warm, as Sera played hopscotch. First she would ride along side of Christina then she would move up beside mike. To Sera it seemed like life just couldn't get any better than this. Every time Sera would ride beside Christina, she would give her a big smile with a twinkle in her big brown eyes that almost looked magical. Back and forth she went all day long. As nighttime grew close, they came upon a working windmill.

*"We will camp here tonight."*

Sera said, as if she was the one that was in charge of the group.

Christina and mike gave each-other a smile, as they watched the glee that Sera was showing as they set camp.

*"I'll go get dinner."*

Mike said, pulling his rifle from the holder on the saddle.

*"Mike; Sera and I were stuck inside that cave a long time, and it really stank, so maybe you will take your time."*

Christina said, holding her fingers up-under her noise and pointing toward the water tank.

*"Not a problem."*

Mike said, turning and giving Christina a wink and a smile, and then headed for the woods.

*"Damn him, when he does that I forget what I was thinking about."*

Christina explained to Sera, then she closed her eyes and listened to Sera giggling loudly.

Christina never has felt this emotion before but, she decided that she really liked the feeling.

Christina and Sera built the camp fire, than took a long deserving shower to wash away all the bad smells from the cave. Then Christina sat, meticulously braiding Sera's long hair, Sera set with her eyes closed, pretending to be a helpless little girl. After Sera had put her ponytails in place, Christina pulled out her dad's favorite book. Sera climbs into Christina's lap and began her reading lesson.

Mike returned from his hunt with the hind quarter of a deer and wild onions, wild potatoes, and a small watermelon. Mike noticed that Sera was reading to Christina from the book of the Holy Bible, as she snuggled into her lap. Christina and Sera glanced up as he walked by and gave his smile and a wink, causing Christina to lose her train of thought, Sera looked up at her with a loud giggle.

When the short reading lesson was over, Christina and Sera joined Mike by the camp fire, watching as he began preparing the meal. Mike would give an occasional glance over at Christina with his wink and a smile, which caused Sera to giggle as she watched Christina's face turn a deep red.

*"I'm going to go and play."*

Sera said, growing board with the hum-dum chore of cooking.

Sera took Big Red to play a game of fetch, as Christina and mike tended to cooking dinner.

*"Mike, I want to thank you for everything; I mean, like saving our lives."*

Christina said with a soft voice, giving Mike an exotic look with her eyes; hoping that she was doing it right and hoping he would notice.

*"I'm always glad to help ladies in distress."*

Mike said, staring into Christina's deep blue eyes.

"Well, I'm very thankful."

Christina said, as she fidgeted with her hair, and then turned to watch Sera and Big Red playing.

"I saw you and Sera reading, most kids don't like to read."

Mike said, carefully removing the food from the fire.

"Yea, Sera couldn't read when we first met, but she learns so fast it's amazing."

Christina said with pride in her voice, as she continued to watch as Sera played with Big Red.

"So, she's not yours?"

Mike asked, with curiosity in his voice and a curious look on his face.

"NO, .No, we met a couple months back, a long story on the two of us."

Christina said, letting her mind drift back through all the memories that the two of them have made together.

"Sounds intriguing; I can't wait to hear it; that is an interesting book you chose to use."

Mike said, setting down beside Christina, causing her mind short circuit.

"You know the book?"

Christina asks, nervously twirling at the ends of in her hair.

"Yes,.. Yes I do, very well in fact, my dad is a preacher."

Mike said proudly, standing and waving for Sera to come eat.

"Well then, I guess me and you do have something in common. My dad was also a preacher."

Christina said, as she got this sensation that seemed to send a warm shock through her body.

Sera came and set down between Mike and Christina, making Mike move over a tad so to make room for her.

"So, what's up with this; ridding with us only a few days?"

Sera asked point blank, curious of whom is and what does Mike do.

"Well young lady, I live about a three days ride east of here."

Mike said, as he started to dish out a meal fit for a king.

Sera sat still, considering his words for just a moment.

"Wait... You mean you have a house?"

Sera asked with raised excitement in her voice, taking the plate that Mike was holding out for her.

"Yes,.. Yes I do."

Mike said, handing Christina her plate than setting back down beside Sera.

"We don't have a house. It's just me and mom, Big Red, and our horses, against the world."

Sera said proudly, and then she straightened up her back and leaned her head against Christina for just a second.

Christina leans over and gently kissed Sera on top of the head. Mike was amazed, watching the two and their tight relationship.

The night had descended upon the trio as Mike rolled his sleeping bag out about 40 feet away from Christina and Sera's tarp-tent. It wasn't long before the night was filled with the sound of a man's sleeping. Christina thought Sera was in a deep sleep, as Sera laid with her back snuggled up against Christina.

"Grandpapa use to snore like that."

Sera whispers, squeezing Christina's arms that held her tight, and then she giggled.

*"So did my dad."*

Christina whispered, as she fought hard not to laugh out loud.

Sera lay still for a few moments, than she begins to speak.

*"Mom,... We need to talk."*

Sera whispered, rolling over to get a good look at Christina eyes.

*"O. K , sweetheart, what's up?"*

Christina asks, with a nerves sounding voice, as she thought about the birds and the bees.

Sera's face was inches from Christina's, when she got a serious look on her face.

*"O. K... Here's the deal mom, you have to stop cursing."*

Sera whispers with a seriously sounding voice, and demanding sound in her voice.

*"Wait, what the hell are you talking about, I don't curse."*

Christina said, reaching over to put Sera's hair behind her ear.

*"Shit, damn it to hell, bastard, shall I go on?"*

Sera sarcastically asked, reaching over and pushing Christina's hair behind her ear.

*"But that's not cursing, that's just English."*

Christina countered, pulling her head back to get a good look at Sera's face.

*"No mom, it is cursing, I don't mind it myself but a good man doesn't like a woman who curses. I know because grandpapa told me."*

Sera said; she could see Christina's eyes were starting to fill with water.

*"Can I sleep on it.?"*

Christina asks, considering how she had just been schooled about men, by a twelve year old.

*"Sure mom, I love you."*

Sera said, turning over and snuggling back up against Christina.

*"And I love you dearly."*

Christina said, wrapping her arms tightly around Sera.

CHRISTINA AND SERA FADE OFF TO SLEEP

The morning was warm, as Christina opens her eyes, being awakened by the sound of running water.

"What the hel…… heck, is that?"

Christina whispers, as she caught herself in the middle of the curse word.

Christina opened the tent, than slowly sticks her head out of the tent. The sun was still just below the horizon but it was light enough to see. Christina looked around the camp; Big Red was lying next to a small fire. She turned her attention toward where the water sound was coming from. Christina gasped at what she saw. She jolted back into the tent. Mike was standing under the water spout in all of his glory. She has never encountered this situation in all of her thirty years. Christina squeezes her eyes closed, as if she was attempting to erase the image. The gesture just confirmed that the image was etched into her mind forever.

"I need to peeeeee."

Sera said, stretching out inside her sleeping bag as she woke up.

"Not right now!"

Christina demanded in a whisper, putting two fingers over Sera's lips.

"What's up mom?"

Sera asked, talking through Christina's two fingers, and then she hears the water stop running.

"OWWWW, I seeeee."

Sera said sarcastically, removing the two fingers Christina held to her lips.

"SHhhh. He can hear you."

Christina commanded, as she and Sera played their fighting game as Christina tries to cover Sera's mouth.

"Mom, he's just taking a sho- O-MY-GOD- you saw him."

Sera said, as she quickly set up and covered her mouth with her hands.

"Be quiet now!"

Christina whispered, pulling Sera's face tight into her bosom.

"Mom, it's not like you have never seen a man; O-MY-GOD.... You are a virgin."

Sera said in a muffled voice, with her face being forcefully buried into Christina.

"Well, aren't you?"

Christina asks, holding Sera tight against her bosom.

"Yea mom, but I'm like twelve years old."

Sera said, pulling away from Christina and looking up into her eyes.

"Well.... I just never got around to it."

Christina explained, as she pulls Sera's face back into her body.

"I am so proud of you, mom."

Sera said, squeezing Christina with a tight hug.

"O. K. Not another word about this."

Christina whispers, releasing Sera from her tight grip.

"Mother--daughter secrete, but I still need to go pee."

Sera said, looking up at Christina with a huge smile.

Christina cautiously, looked out of the tent door; Mike had his jeans on.

"O. K.- Go."

Christina said, quickly moving out of the way of Sera's escape.

Sera moved like a bullet toward the closes tree and disappeared.

Christina walks straight to the fire, avoiding eye contact with Mike.

"Would you like some coffee?"

Mike asked, retrieving another tin cup from his saddlebag.

*"Yes, thank you."*

Christina said, trying her best to hide the blushing in her cheeks.

*"Are you alright?"*

Mike asked, noticing a slight difference in the way Christina was acting.

Christina kept her eyes on the cup as her mind just kept rerunning the image of Mike's beautiful firm muscled body through her head.

*"Yes ~Yes, I'm just having some kind of weird feelings going-on this morning."*

Christina said, looking up and giving a wink and a smile, toward mike.

Christina looked back down into her cup; she has never done that before, ever. She wondered if that she may have crossed an imaginary line.

*"If we ride hard today, we can get to my house by tomorrow."*

Mike said, as he refilled his cup and then Christina's cup.

*"I need a good hard ride,-.-I can't believe I just said that."*

Christina said, turning her face away from Mike's view, in the attempt to hide her embarrassment.

Mike got a big smile on his face. He stood and began to pack camp. Christina began to help, avoiding eye contact with mike. With everything packed up, and everybody mounted upon their horses, Christina looks at Mike. He gives her a wink and a smile, Sera gave a loud giggle as she looks at Christina.

They kept a fast pace through the day. The sun had reached its peak up in the sky when they came across a working windmill, so they took a break. Christina decides to use this opportunity to interrogate Mike.

*"Do you have family waiting at home?"*

Christina asked, as she sat down beside Mike, watching his expression.

*"You could put it that way."*

Mike answers, pouring himself a cup of cold coffee.

*"Kids?"*

Christina cunningly asked, continuing with her inquisition of Mike.

*"There are lots of Kids."*

Mike said, being very vague with his answers which agitated Christina.

"O.K. So, you have lots of kids."

Christina said, looking at Mike, hoping for some clarity.

*"You will see."*

Mike said, finishing up his coffee and then mounting his horse.

"Is your house safe from U.N. DEMON'S?"

Christina asks, putting her foot in the stirrup to mount BLACKWALL, and then waited for an answer.

"My house is safe from all DEMON'S."

Mike said, giving his best smile and a wink.

Throughout the rest of the day Christina concentrated on the conversation she had with Mike. Someone is waiting at home with lots of kids, Mike did not seem too eager to indulge very much information. Christina imagined a one room cabin, a wife, and five kids surrounded by 20 U. N. DEMON'S. Then her mind drifted over to Mike's sexy smile and his hypnotizing wink, and she lost all of her train of thought. Christina was thankful today's journey was over. Setting camp helped take her mind off of her daydreams about Mike.

Camp was now set, Mike insisted on delegating the hunt, as Christina and Sera did their bathing, then Sera's hair braiding then a little reading. Christina took more time with her own hair this evening. Then the girls set by the fire and watched Mike cook. Dinner was always better when Mike was doing the cooking. By the time they had finished dinner it was after dark.

*"I'm going to bed."*

Sera said, giving Christina a hug and a kiss, and then she gave Mike a kiss on the cheek as she gave him a tight hug.

Christina desperately wanted to learn so much more about this handsome man that has her feeling things she has never known existed. She set beside Mike, and then she began to pick her questions carefully.

*"So, Mike, you have family at home?"*

Christina asks curiously, trying to pry as much information out of Mike as possible.

*"No blood family, but there are some people that I consider as family."*

Mike said, deciding that he may like the idea of having this beautiful woman for his wife.

*"So, no living family?"*

Christina asks, as she twirled the ends of her hair.

*"Yes, my parents have a small farm about two weeks ride east of my place."*

Mike said, pouring Christina and himself a cup of coffee.

*"Let me guess, their names are Mary and Joe, and they have chickens."*

Christina jokingly said with a slight giggle, knowing she was completely wrong.

*"Yes, you have met them?"*

Mike asks, with a surprise in his voice as he stares at Christina.

**"ASK HIM IF HE IS MARRIED."**

Sera screamed out from inside of her tent.

Sera was growing a little aggravated with all of Christina's beating around the bush questions. Christina turned and looked toward the tent, as she feels the flash of warmth running through her body.

*"Never married."*

Mike said, loud enough so that Sera would hear.

**"YES!"**

Sera screamed once again, as she continues to listens to their conversation.

*"I'm sorry, It's just she had a dream that you were her father."*

Christina explains, turning back with a smile on her face.

*"Well, I did make an impression on her back at the Cave."*

Mike said with a chuckle, refilling his coffee cup.

*"No, before that Mike, it's kind of hard to explain but Sera and I have these dreams, and sometimes these dreams will come true."*

Christina said slowly, hoping that he would not think that she was a crazy woman.

*"OH, I see, and do **you**, ever dream about me?"*

Mike asks, looking toward Christina with one of his famous, winks and cute smile.

*"Not when I'm sleeping."*

Christina said, closing her eyes, than wished she could somehow turn back time for at least five seconds.

*"So, tell me how you met my mom and dad."*

Mike said, in order to change the subject, seeing Christina's embarrassment.

*"They gave me shelter, and let me sleep in their barn one stormy night."*

Christina said, thankful that Mike changed the subject.

*"If you'd been there for the Sabbath, you would have enjoyed that."*

Mike said, rolling his sleeping bag out onto the ground.

*"I was. So tell me Mike, what are you doing way out here so far from home?"*

Christina asked, still trying to find out what it is about this man that keeps her so preoccupied.

*"I was looking for you."*

Mike said, giving a curious look, as to the Sabbath question.

*"Mike; Are you having dreams about me?"*

Christina asks, giving Mike a wink and a smile.

*"NO; No, nothing like that, I travel around this part of the country looking to find good descent people to come join our little community. Over the years I have managed to get thirty couples, most with kids. Maybe you and Sera will join us."*

Mike explained, taking a seat on top of the sleeping bag.

**"YES! YES!"**

Sera yells, as she is over come with joy at the idea of a genuine family.

*"Mike, I don't think I can be living with a man that I'm not married to. I have to consider what Sera would think."*

Christina explained, turning and looking up at the stars; trying to keep control of her breathing.

*"You and Sera will have your own room, and come spring, we will go to visit my parents, and there might be a wedding."*

Mike said, as he lay looking up toward the stars.

*"MIKE!! Are you asking me to marry you?"*

Christina asks with a shaky voice, she could feel a fluttering deep down in her stomach.

*"Well, not today, but maybe someday."*

Mike said, looking toward Christina with a wink and a smile.

**"YES!! YES!! YES!!"**

Sera's voice, echoed through the forest as she began to laugh with joy.

*"I better go and get her to sleep. Goodnight Mike, sweet dreams."*

Christina said, as she gave Mike a wink and a smile, and then went to the tent where Sera was still giggling.

The morning was perfect as the sun rose, they were on their way. Christina and Sera, began to sing songs as they rode along, anticipating on their arrival. Around mid afternoon, Big Red came running fast down the trail, as he ran up to Christina he gave one of his whisper barks.

"*Someone is up ahead.*"

Christina said, pulling BLACKWALL to a halt.

"*It's O.K., they are some of my people.*"

Mike assured Christina, and kept riding up the trail.

Christina settles Big Red down assuring him that everything was good. Four men approached from up the trail, each wearing a gun.

"*Boss man, I'm glad to see your home.*"

One of the men said, as they rode around behind and began to follow.

"*Boss man?*"

Christina asks, giving a curious look over at Mike.

"*Yea, this is my land, my community.*"

Mike said, giving Christina a wink and a smile.

The trail became wide and level, as if well traveled. Houses began to dot the road side as the town came into view, Sera became all excited.

*"Mom look, a real town, with stores and houses, a school, a real school."*

Sera said, as she kept looking at all of the different stores that lined the street.

They turned down a long drive lined with tall trees. At the end of the driveway, they came up to a big ranch house, with a rap around porch, and a porch swing. Behind the house they could see the huge garden, with all the vegetables.

## "H O M E"

# TAKE MY HAND
## BY- RAYDON COOLEY

IT FEELS JUST LIKE HEAVEN
WHEN YOU'RE LYING NEXT TO ME
YOU REMIND ME OF AN ANGLE
WHEN I'M WATCHING WHILE YOU SLEEP
YOUR TOUCH BURNS LIKE FIRE
FROM THE DEEPEST PITS OF HELL
YOU SET MY SOLE ON FIRE
WITH THE LOVING THAT YOU GIVE
TAKE MY HAND
LET'S WALK THROUGH LIFE TOGETHER
THESE UPS AND DOWNS
WE WILL MAKE IT THROUGH
WHEN THE ROAD GETS ROUGH
AND YOU START TO GET WEARY
YOU CAN LEAN ON ME
AND I'LL LEAN ON YOU
SKIN SOFT AS VELVET
SO GENTLE TO THE TOUCH
LOVE AS WARM AS SUNSHINE
I CAN NEVER GET ENOUGH
YOU ARE MY RAINBOW
I FOUND MY POT OF GOLD
YOU ARE MY SHELTER
FROM THE COLD WIND WHEN SHE BLOWS

# CHAPTER 15
## THE BIG PLAN

When the weather began to warm, Christina, Sera and Mike made the trip to his parent's house. Mary and Joe were overly excited to see Christina with Mike, and fell in love with Sera. In mid-march Christina and Mike were married. Sera could not control her giggling as she walked down the aisle and spread the flowers out onto the ground in front of Christina as she slowly walked beside Joe. Mikes and Christina were very surprised that about fifty people from Mikesville attended the wedding at his parent's house.

Sera now works as the elementary school teacher. She would constantly read, and with her photographic memory she was even tutoring some of the high school students. Sera was so excited on Christmas day, all she could do was sit and cry, as Christina delivered her a very special Christmas present; A BABY BROTHER.

Mike has put together a brigade of twenty well armed men and women to go with him on his trips to gather others to join their town. On long trips like going to Debby's, Christina and Sera would insist on coming alone. Sera always insisted that her little brother Joshua come with.

After a few years, Christina had all her friends that she had made throughout her journey with her in Mikesville.

## "THE BIG PLAN"

CHRISTINA WHISPERS.

## THE END

Made in the USA
Middletown, DE
27 April 2017